BABE IN PARADISE

fiction

MARISA SILVER

W. W. Norton & Company New York London

Copyright © 2001 by Marisa Silver

Printed in the United States of America
First published as a Norton paperback 2002

"The Passenger," "What I Saw from Where I Stood," and "Gunsmoke" first
appeared in *The New Yorker.* "Babe in Paradise" first appeared in *The Georgetown
Review.* "Falling Bodies" first appeared in *The Beloit Fiction Journal.* "What I Saw
from Where I Stood" also appeared in *Best American Short Stories 2001.*

For information about permission to reproduce selections from this book,
write to Permissions, W. W. Norton & Company, Inc., 500 Fifth Avenue,
New York, NY 10110

The text of this book is composed in Bembo with the display set in
Officina Sans Book
Composition by Molly Heron
Manufacturing by The Haddon Craftsmen, Inc.
Book design by Chris Welch
Production manager: Julia Druskin

Library of Congress Cataloging-in-Publication Data
Silver, Marisa.
    Babe in paradise: fiction / Marisa Silver
        p. cm.
    Contents: Babe in paradise—Two criminals—What I saw from where I stood—
Statues—Thief—Falling bodies—Gunsmoke—The missing—The passenger.
    ISBN 0-393-02003-7
    1. Los Angeles (Calif.)—Fiction. I. Title
PS3619.I55B342001
813'.54—dc21   2001018314
    ISBN 0-393-32384-6 pbk.

W. W. Norton & Company, Inc., 500 Fifth Avenue, New York, N.Y. 10110
www.wwnorton.com

W. W. Norton & Company Ltd., Castle House, 75/76 Wells Street,
London WIT 3QT

1 2 3 4 5 6 7 8 9 0

"Painfully real characters and strikingly inventive writing."
— *Publishers Weekly*

"Reserved, elegant writing."   — *Hartford Courant*

"How well Marisa Silver writes about her ne'er-do-well characters, and how cunningly she invents their lives in these glittering stories. *Babe in Paradise* is a passionate and memorable debut."   — Margot Livesey

"Marisa Silver writes about the margins, where loss, profit, hunger, and generosity lie beside each other like Silver's lovers, pressing hard but doomed to be separate. She tells these stories with honesty, and also with mercy; you end up believing that she cares for these people as much as you do."
— Frederick Busch

FOR KEN, HENRY, AND OLIVER

CONTENTS

ACKNOWLEDGMENTS

Many thanks to Geoffrey Wolff, Antonya Nelson, and Robert Boswell, generous readers and critics. Thanks to Judith Erlich, Daniel Stern, and especially Hilma Wolitzer for their encouragement and help along the way. Heartfelt thanks to Bill Buford and Meghan O'Rourke. Thanks to Kristina Loggia and Racelle Schaefer for their faith, their examples, and their boys. Enormous thanks to Henry Dunow, Jill Bialosky, and to Joan, Ray, Dina, and Claudia.

And finally, thanks to Ken, for everything.

BABE IN PARADISE

The hills were on fire. Babe stood high up on a ladder and flung a bucket of water across the shingles of her roof. She handed the pail down to Delia, her mother, who stood below on the ground. The night was dark. No stars shone through the thick layer of blackness. The only illumination came from the flashlight Delia trained on the roof, its orb bobbing unsteadily under her nervous guidance. The beam of light slid down off the house and traveled across the lawn with Delia as she moved to fill the pail from the outside spigot. Then she slowly made her way back to the ladder, her thin frame listing with the load. She rested the bucket on the ground and looked up at her daughter. Babe tried to ignore the anxious set of her mother's face and the way Delia repeatedly bit into her lower lip. Carefully, she climbed down the ladder to retrieve the water.

Babe felt the tight grab of her new green army jacket under her arms as she descended. It was not her jacket, really, but one she had stolen from the Goodwill truck that morning. Before that, it belonged to someone named Thompson or Thomas; the big black letters read "Thom," but the rest had been scraped away by nervous fingers or too many washings. Babe thought about this Thompson/Thomas, whether he was fat or thin, long-haired or short. She inhaled the material to see if she could detect the scent of another body, but all she smelled was the musky odor of smoke. In the distance, a black ball, like a roll of dirty cotton, hung in the sky.

"There have always been fires and there will always be fires," Delia announced frantically, drawing her wet fingers through her hair. "People survive them. Most people do."

"The fire is nowhere near us," Babe said, climbing up the ladder with the full bucket. "On TV they said it won't even jump the break."

"Unless the winds change. We should have started hours ago."

"We don't even own this dump," Babe said wearily. "Why are we trying to save it?"

"We've got first and last and a deposit in it. This house is our bank account, Baby. This is all we've got."

Babe heaved the bucket onto the roof. Water splashed over her, raining down on the ground below. Her mother shrieked and lifted her flowered skirt high above her knees. Deep purple veins traveled up and down her dark thighs, varicose reminders of her age and her pregnancy, sixteen years before. Still, her body moved like a dancer's, with a fluency that eluded Babe's own rounded, ungraceful figure. People often commented on Delia's fragile beauty—like a flower, they said, or a china doll. Unable to find her imprint in her mother's face or body, Babe imagined she must resemble her father, but she would never know this for sure; he'd left before Babe was born. She collected photographs of every place she and her mother had lived in, keeping them in an antique box—the only thing of real value they owned. But there were no photographs of this man.

Babe tilted the nearly empty bucket over her head, rubbing the remaining water on her face and smearing her red lipstick onto her hands. She had spent her first few teenage years hiding her outsized mouth and full lips behind her hand or by keeping her shoulders hunched and her head down. But since moving to Los Angeles, where beauty assaulted her everywhere she looked, she had decided to wear only the boldest colors she could find on discount. Her skin was pale, and when she rimmed her eyes with dark kohl, and wore her red or purple or sometimes even black lipsticks, her ugliness became a challenge. Kids kept their distance. This was the way she liked it.

Dripping with water, she pulled her damp shirt away from her chest. She smelled of the mingled odors of sex, Rockport's skin, and his Goodwill truck she'd been in only hours earlier, straddling his skinny, naked body. She'd worn the army jacket and nothing else.

———

He'd said "I love you," which only meant he was done. So Babe rolled off him onto a mound of mildewed clothes. He tried to finish her off with his hand while she stared into the gunmetal-gray truck ceiling. First and second period were over and if she came quickly, she could sneak into study hall without anybody noticing she was late. But even though she tried thinking about climbing a mountain, then about a sleazy film she'd seen on late-night cable, nothing happened.

"Forget it," she said, slipping out from beneath him. His concave chest and narrow hips accentuated her own broadness, although she was the healthier-looking of the two. His skin was tinged with gray. She often wondered if he ever left his truck at all. She knew nothing about him except that he was thirty-two years old, her mother's age. She didn't even know his whole name.

"I gotta get out of here," she announced. "Give me a rag or something. Something clean."

He pulled a plaid cotton shirt from the bed of clothes beneath him and held it up to her. "There's a secret history to this shirt," he mused. "Think of its life, what it's seen."

"It's a fucking shirt," she snapped, grabbing it from him and pushing it between her legs. "Are you a freak?" she added. "Am I fucking a retard?"

He smiled as he stood up to get his half-empty beer can from the back of the truck. His penis, long and half swollen, dangled between his legs. Babe turned away. The bodies of men embarrassed her, and she often rushed into sex to avoid having to look at them. With her eyes closed and her head buried in someone's neck, she could almost convince herself she was alone. She stood up and began to dress.

"You're beautiful," he said, coming towards her with his beer.

"Liar," she said, repulsed by the idea that she had, once again, allowed him inside her body. He lay back down on his mattress of discarded clothes, his head nested in his crossed arms. The sparse tufts of black hair in his armpits looked like flowers after a nuclear holocaust. She sucked in her stomach in order to button her tight jeans, then cinched her belt so her flesh plumped over the sides.

"I'm here all week," he said, smiling up at her. "Then I'm in Sunland for I don't know how long."

"Then I probably won't see you. I have things to do." She enjoyed the look of uncertainty that flashed across his face but her pleasure quickly soured into disgust. His need repulsed her. She felt this conflict of desires too when he stroked her with his long, lean fingers, as if she were something worth touching. It made her want to scream.

"It's so easy to make boys love you," she said. "All you have to do is spread your legs."

By the time Babe and her mother had circled the entire house with the ladder and bucket, the section of roof they had watered first was nearly dry. This fact only encouraged Delia's growing panic. Babe knew the fire was a confirmation of everything her mother feared: that the world was an unwelcoming place, and that their life was barely hinged to its periphery. As far as Babe could tell, her mother lived tautly, waiting for the next deliverance of bad luck. When it arrived, she met it with equal degrees of astonishment and resignation. Delia had become obsessed by disaster, fearing the mud slides, quakes, and fires which afflicted the city like recurring diseases. She lived with the daily assumption that something terrible would happen, an expectation so fierce it bordered on hope. Babe was surprised that her mother had chosen to move to this city at all. But Delia was worn out from failing in so many cold and lightless midwestern cities. Los Angeles held out the possibility of paradise.

"Can you smell it, Baby?" Delia called up the ladder, her voice constricted by fear. "I'd rather die than wait like this. I'd rather die and get it over with."

"I don't smell anything," Babe said evenly, although she did—the air had filled up with the fire's sweet scent. Still, she had to remain calm in the face of her mother's rising anxiety. She climbed down the ladder and repositioned it under the next dry patch of roof. "Fill a bucket," she commanded.

"Twenty-five houses have been consumed. Think of those poor people, Baby. They have nothing left. Can you imagine? Baby, can you?"

"Don't freak out on me, Mother. I'm not kidding."

"I won't," Delia whimpered apologetically and carried the full bucket back to the ladder. "Cross my heart."

"Let's keep going," Babe said, hoping that, if she could keep her mother focused, Delia might not have one of her fits.

Her mother called them "episodes," as if they were television shows, momentarily transfixing but instantly forgettable.

Babe was unable to forget. First came a low, wandering drone that Babe almost always mistook for a hurt animal until she located it coming from deep within her mother's chest. Next, Delia's eyes would fasten on some nonspecific place in the room, as if the world had consolidated into a fraction of air. Babe would call out, but her mother would not respond. If Babe tried to bring Delia out of her trance by touching her, she'd get no reaction at all. She'd have to wait—seconds, if the fit was mild; minutes, if it was not. Finally, the hum would sub-side and Delia would fall into a deep, childlike sleep. Babe would stand vigil nearby, afraid to turn on the television for fear of waking her mother, scared her mother might not wake at all. She'd make halfhearted attempts at cleaning the kitchen or straightening the living room—activities she would nor-mally avoid. The rest of the time, she would sit on Delia's bed and watch the slow, twitching breaths quiver across her mother's chest.

Delia's fits were always followed by a state of temporary amnesia. Waking, she would forget the fit, her name, even the name of her own daughter. It was up to Babe to remind her mother of their life. She would take old photographs out of her box and describe the many places they had lived. But in all her recollections, she omitted the memories that haunted her dreams. She did not remind her mother of the apartment in St. Louis where Babe, age eight, had waited alone each night for her mother to return from her job at a bar, her alertness her only defense against the intruders she was certain lurked outside the door. Neither did she tell her mother that the man photographed steadying Babe on a pony in Muncie was also the one who slipped into bed beside her one night, exploring her body until she bit him.

Instead, Babe told of their visit to a gem cave on the way from Missouri to Ohio, or about the giant crab-shaped crab house somewhere in New England. Finally, Delia's face would brighten with recognition. "You're an amazing girl," she would say to Babe as she emerged from her oblivion, fresh and hopeful as a newborn. "You remember everything."

A doctor's diagnosis in St. Louis: panic disorder. The cure: tranquilizers Delia complained about and quickly lost. So the fits continued, each one signaling a time to move on. Soon after one, they would pack their belongings, place the key under the doormat, avoiding landlords or unsatisfied lovers, and leave. "Forget everything that's ever happened to you," Delia would tell Babe as they drove towards their next home. "Your life begins now."

When Babe finished emptying the last bucket of water onto the roof, she went inside the house. The television was on and Delia was pulling a large red suitcase down from the closet shelf.

"We're going to have to evacuate," Delia said, lowering the case to the floor.

"Says who?"

"Just look at the TV."

Babe watched the screen as a house crumbled underneath the weight of flames. "Carbon Canyon," a newscaster's voice intoned. "Consumed."

"That's miles away," she sighed, sitting heavily on the worn couch.

The phone rang and Delia gasped as she answered, as if expecting the fire to announce itself on the other end of the line. But when her voice mellowed, Babe knew that one of the mothers was calling.

"Are you holding the baby in the football position?" Delia said slowly. "Did you ram his head onto your boob?" She listened for a few moments. Delia worked as a lactation consultant, renting breast pumps out of her car and administering advice to nursing mothers. Babe was astonished that her mother was trusted by people she hardly knew. "Keep trying," Delia continued, gently. "Don't cry. Of course you're a good mother."

As she listened to the soothing patter, Babe's neck and jaw grew tight. She had to suppress the urge to scream or grab the phone and fling it at her mother. She turned over on her stomach and found a pen buried between the cushions. She wrote her name in small precise letters on the palm of her hand, pressing hard so that the skin became white and bloodless. She considered writing Rockport's name next to her own, maybe enclosing both within a heart. But she knew the emotions she had for him were not love, and that someone who encouraged such feelings of disgust and petulant wanting did not love her either.

She met Rockport six months earlier when she dropped items off at his Goodwill truck. Her garbage bag was full of things

Delia had not been able to sell—snow boots from St. Louis, an Indians hat from their months in Cleveland, a pair of black patent-leather Mary Janes with worn-down heels. Since the Goodwill truck was parked only a block from Babe's high school, it had been up to her to drop off the bag. Her plan was to deliver the bag, cut school, and patrol the mall until two-thirty. She'd thumb a ride up the canyon when it was time to go home.

When Rockport first appeared at the gate of the truck, Babe thought he was the ugliest man she'd ever seen. His face was thin, his eyes watchful and untrusting. Acne scars ran down each cheek, unpitying souvenirs of childhood.

"Anything edible?" he said, opening the trash bag.

She thought she had surprised a scavenger and looked at his hands, expecting them to be dirty and ravaged. Instead, his fingers were long and delicate, his nails the color of chalk. "No," she said, confused. "Are you hungry?"

He smiled knowingly, then upended the bag onto the bed of the truck. "Food carries bacteria. Bacteria makes disease. Goodwill is in the business of helping people, not sending them to their graves."

She watched, horrified, as a pair of her old cotton underpants fell out last, a splotch of faded red hearts landing on top of the great polyglot pile.

"We're not picky at the Goodwill," he said, noticing the direction of her gaze. "You think the people who get your panties care whose ass was in them first?"

She wanted to leave but he offered her a beer. She took his hand and climbed into the dark interior of the truck, where a radio, hot plate, mattress, and a green BarcaLounger combined into a makeshift home. The order of his belongings surprised her. Shoes rested in boxes, shirts were folded neatly on top of a milk crate. When he turned away to get her drink, she looked closely at a pile of books stacked in the corner. She picked up a ragged paperback with a drawing of a heavily armored, big-busted alien on its cover.

"I hate science fiction," she said, tossing the book onto the mattress.

"The past and the future are the only places where your life can really happen," he said, handing her the beer.

"Bullshit. Your life can't happen in the past."

"This is where you're wrong. You can reinvent yourself in your memories. You could say you were anyone. Who would know?"

She eyed him warily. "You're not some crystal freak, are you?" she asked.

He laughed, the creases on his face deepening. "No. I just have a lot of time on my hands. It's good to have a visitor."

"I'm not a visitor. I don't even know you."

"Would you like to?"

"That's lame," she said, grinning despite herself.

"Well, would you?"

"No."

The first time they had sex, he did not have a rubber, so he pulled out of her. He asked her to finish him off with her hand, but she said no. What he wanted made her uncomfortable and required a kind of intimacy she could not bear. She'd been having sex for two years and had slept with four different boys. They were often drunk and did not so much touch her as wash over her like indistinct waves. The sex was fast and practical and the boys always seemed surprised when they realized it was over. Their astonishment gave Babe a sense of power: she could get a boy off and do it quickly. Sex was the very first thing she was good at.

"Babe!" Delia cried, waking Babe, who sat up on the couch groggily, surprised that she had drifted off. Her mother stared at the television, holding a hand over her mouth. A woman reporter in a yellow slicker gesticulated wildly in front of a ball of fire which twisted on the ground like a whirl of leaves. When Babe looked closely, the fire turned out to be a burning dog. The animal performed a frenzied dance as it attempted to knock off the cape of flames. Finally, a fireman threw himself on top of the animal until the fire was extinguished. The dog lay, charred and motionless, on the ground.

"It's dead," Delia whimpered. Her eyes dropped from the screen until they fixed on the carpet below.

"Let's check the roof," Babe said automatically, trying to keep her mother from slipping into the vortex of her fears. "Get the flashlight. Mom, can you hear me?"

"Yes," her mother answered faintly.

"In the closet, Mom. Go. Now."

Outside, Delia tried to light Babe's way to the roof, but her anxiety made her inattentive. Babe climbed the ladder, searching for rungs in the dark. Reaching the top, she found the shingles were dry. The smoky hot air entered her nostrils, constricting her throat and chest. She realized the fire was close, and that her efforts were useless now. She looked out across the canyon. A dusty haze obscured the new moon, leaving not darkness, but a vacancy of light. The trees stood still in the windless air.

Suddenly a dull, dense sound of encroaching thunder rose up out of the woods and converged on the yard. The noise became deafening when a herd of deer, barely visible in the darkness, burst out of the trees and raced across the lawn. Their movement created a wind so strong that the ladder swayed underneath Babe. She hugged the shingles and felt the vibration of hooves penetrate her chest. Delia's flashlight gleamed over the animals' dark bodies. Babe could see the shiny wetness of their eyes, and how they moved with a mindless will, as though someone had given them the signal to run, but had not told them where to, or why.

The silence that followed the animals' disappearance was expectant and dangerous. Somewhere inside its vastness rose Delia's wandering hum.

Babe worked quickly. She sat her mother in the Toyota, then ran back into the house, where she threw clothes into a suitcase, grabbed the box of photos and her mother's purse, and dragged everything back outside. The news reports had warned of looters roaming the abandoned hills, so she left the lights and TV on. She piled everything into the trunk of the car and started to drive.

Once off their small street, they joined the slow line of vehicles moving down the main road of the canyon. Motorcycles darted in and out between cars, stealing ahead in line and causing anxious drivers to honk their horns. Dogs rode unchained in the beds of trucks, trapped between suitcases and boxes overflowing with hastily collected possessions. Sirens wailed, signaling the imminent approach of fire engines, but when they appeared, they inched their way up the crowded, winding road, slow as toys.

"On the news, they're going to be talking about how many people died," Delia said, bunching and unbunching the material of her dress. "They're going to be saying 'Twenty people died,' or 'Fifty people died.'"

"Calm down, Mom," Babe said, her stomach tightening as she noticed the work of her mother's hands.

"Let's sing," Delia said. She tapped her foot quickly on the floorboards. "Something we both know. Think, Baby. I can't remember a thing."

"A, my name is Alice . . . " Babe began, recalling the endless chant that had eased the boredom of their cross-country drives, ". . . and my husband's name is—"

"Albert!"

"We live in Albany, and we sell—"

"Alfalfa!"

Babe drove carefully around a stopped car which had been driven partway off the road and abandoned. A hundred feet ahead, a family walked down the canyon road. The parents carried suitcases. The children, wearing their colorful school backpacks, clasped stuffed animals and blankets to their chests. When an emergency worker in an orange vest tried to direct the family back to its forsaken car, the father pushed him away with such violence that the man fell onto the pavement.

"B, my name is—"

"Bonnie!" Delia said, pounding out the beat of the rhyme on the dashboard with her fist.

Forty-five minutes later, they reached the bottom of the canyon. The road was a fairground of flashing red and yellow emergency lights. People ran in all directions, shouting orders into the night. The northbound side of the street was blocked off, so Babe followed the line of cars going the other direction. Twenty minutes later, they arrived in the parking lot of her school.

They parked and entered the gym, which was set up as a temporary shelter. Delia clutched her purse and the box of photographs, Babe carried the suitcase and a breast pump, which, in her haste, she had pulled from the trunk of the car.

"This is where you play your sports?" Delia said distract-edly. She had only been to the registration office at the school once in order to sign Babe's transfer forms.

"It smells like it too," Babe said, sickened by the odors of bodies and sweat and food. The gym reverberated with the noise of a hundred displaced people. Red Cross cots stretched from one end of the room to the other, most of them already claimed by families. As soon as Babe located two free cots, she placed their belongings around them proprietarily and lay down. Delia put the box of photos between their cots, then opened the suitcase and began to unpack.

"This isn't a hotel," Babe said, glancing at her mother.

"I had the idea these were suffocating in the suitcase," Delia said, fanning a shirt in the air. "It will be hard to get the burny smell out. Smoke lingers."

Babe shut her eyes while her mother organized and grunted her assent when Delia said she was going to find the bathroom. Fifteen minutes later, Delia returned with two paper plates heaped with spaghetti. After they had eaten and Delia had fallen asleep, Babe wrote a note on a scrap of paper, placed it on Delia's chest, and left the gym.

She banged on the side of the Goodwill truck, and after a few moments, Rockport opened the rear doors. He wore only a pair of striped shorts.

"Our house is burning up," she said, taking his hand and climbing into the truck. Sitting on the chair, she watched while he finished a plate of rice and beans. A pair of little girl's sparkling red slippers lay at the foot of Rockport's mattress. She reached for them.

"Somebody dropped those off today," he said, wiping his mouth with the palm of his hand. "I'm going to send them to my daughter."

"You have a daughter?" Babe asked. She never thought of Rockport with a life outside the truck.

"Daughter, wife, condo in the Valley. The whole shebang." He took a framed photograph from underneath a pile of his shirts and handed it to Babe. The child in the picture was perhaps eight or nine, blond, like the woman beside her, but with eyes as dark and suspicious as her father's. Babe ran her fingers along the heavy silver frame.

"Wedding present," he said. "The money's all hers. I miss the kid."

"Go and see her. Who's stopping you?"

He wagged his finger in the air. "Restraining order. Like a leash. I went a little crazy on my wife. I fucked up her face pretty good."

She looked at his hands. The palms seemed twice the size of her own, his fingers long and menacing as tentacles. Babe realized anything could happen to her. No one knew where she was.

"My wife's filling my little girl with bull, you can bet on that," Rockport said, anger distorting his mouth. "There's so much crap that goes into making things turn out wrong. It's not just one thing, right? My wife wakes up one day and says, 'Sayonara, baby.' What kind of shit is that?" Suddenly he twisted around and slammed his fist into the side of the truck. The sound reverberated like thunder. Then he turned back and fixed a penetrating gaze on Babe.

"Babe," he said darkly. "What's your real name?"

She started backing up towards the doors. "That's it. What you see is what you get," she said, trying to disguise her exit with chatter. "It's really 'Baby Girl Ellis,' like it says on the hospital bracelet. My mother couldn't think of anything better. I can choose my own name whenever I want. She doesn't want the responsibility."

He moved towards her as she spoke. His eyes lit up with delight. She could not tell whether it was her story that had entertained him or the prospect of her entrapment. Just as she was about to turn and run, he grabbed her shoulders.

"Rita," he said, holding her close, his warm musty breath clogging her nostrils.

"What?" Her stomach lurched as he pulled her down to the truck bed.

"I'm naming you. Rita. Or Margaret."

"I have to go."

He kissed her face, her neck, her breasts. "Or Jane. Lady Jane. Or Persephone. That's from a myth. Do you like it?"

"Stop," she said, weakly.

He moved down her legs, biting her thighs through her jeans. "Rachel," he said. "Raquelle." His hands reached up and teased at the skin of her waist. "I'll give you a name." He ran his tongue along her belly where her shirt parted from her jeans. "Dolores," he said, exhaling heavily. "Girl of my sorrow."

She thought she would explode, that every hideous feeling she had of wanting and hating him would spill out of her. She climbed down on the floor beside him and quickly undid the button and zipper of his shorts. Reaching inside, she watched as his face grew helpless. She pushed her own jeans and underwear down around her boots and pulled him into her.

After he came, he lay behind her, his chest moving in and out against her back.

"You didn't use anything," she said, feeling his wetness between her thighs. "You're supposed to pull out."

"I forgot."

"Fuck that," she said angrily, standing and pulling up her clothes. He lay below her with his eyes closed. His body stuttered, still possessed by the sex. The silver-framed photograph had somehow ended up next to his head, making it look as though he were part of the family portrait, except that his face was grotesquely outsized compared to his discarded wife's and child's. She wanted to spit on him.

BABE IN PARADISE   29

"You think your wife and your kid talk about you," she said. "But they don't. To them, you don't even exist."

He smiled mockingly, not opening his eyes. "Hmmm," he murmured. "Are you still here?"

Heat flooded her body. She lifted up her foot and kicked his sickening, unsuspecting face with the hard toe of her boot. For a moment, she heard nothing. Then the sound of his piercing scream filled the truck. She jumped down off the back gate and ran into the night.

When she returned to the gym, her mother was not on her cot. Babe noticed a crowd gathered in a corner and began walking towards it. She felt numb as she imagined people witnessing her mother in the throes of a fit. But when she reached the group she realized it was really a loose circle of people clapping and dancing. Delia and a man Babe did not recognize moved to music from a cordless radio. Delia spun freely, her flowered skirt fanning out into a perfect circle. A delighted smile spread across her face.

Exhausted, Babe turned from the crowd and went to her cot. When she sat down, she noticed that the antique box was missing.

"That was fun," Delia said, returning and sitting on her cot. "People here are so nice. I'll tell you, now that the worst has happened, I feel so much better. Isn't that strange?"

"Where are the photos?" Babe said.

Her mother looked down at the empty space on the floor. "They were here," she said, alarmed. "I put them right there."

"Somebody ripped us off."

"No. That can't be."

"They took the box. Somebody stole our fucking box."

Babe walked through the rows of cots, scanning the piles of belongings stacked alongside the beds. She asked a few people about the box, describing it in great detail, but no one was interested or claimed to have seen it.

"Who's going to say they have our box?" she said to her mother when she returned. "That would be admitting they stole it."

"We'll get the pictures back, Baby. I know we will."

"No, we won't. We won't get them back. They're gone. Don't you get it?" Babe said, frustrated by her mother's naïveté.

Delia sighed. "Those were such nice pictures too. The one of you on the pony? Remember?"

Wetness rimmed Babe's eyes. "I have to sleep," she said. "All I want to do is sleep."

By dawn the next day, the fires had been contained. Babe and Delia drove back up the canyon. They ran the windshield wipers to clear off the thin mist of ash which fell on the car like black snow. Delia made Babe stop several times so she could lean out the passenger window to ask emergency workers for information about their street, but no one could tell her whether the house had survived the night. As they drove on, vistas opened out that were once wooded and close but now boasted trees scorched bare by flames. Smoke floated a few feet above the ground like a layer of fog. Babe had the sensation she was in a place she'd never been before, a place so ancient it had no history, so ruined nothing could ever grow there.

"Oh, dear," Delia said softly. "So much death."

At the turnoff to their street, Babe felt an urge to pass by and simply press on to the next city. She wanted to hear her mother say "Our life begins now!" in that unreasonably assured way of hers.

"Oh, Babe." Delia shuddered. "Look."

The fire had played a random game of chance with their street, burning some houses, sparing others. Theirs had been unlucky. The front half was gone, burned completely off. Only the back hallway and the two bedrooms were left standing, fully exposed like a doll's house. Most of the furniture and all their possessions were either destroyed or singed to an unrecognizable blackness.

Babe and Delia stepped out of the car into a bed of ash. As they walked towards what was once their kitchen, their shoes sent up a thick powder which settled on their faces and arms. Odd things survived—a fork, Delia's metal worry beads, one stove burner. Babe began to dig through the rubble, collecting stray items. Delia wandered away and sat down on the stone hearth of what was their living room. She shuffled a worry bead slowly back and forth between her hands as she looked out across the ruined house.

"There's nothing," Delia said. "Not one thing."

Her voice was weak, but Babe did not see signs of an oncoming fit. Delia was simply defeated. Babe realized, sadly, that her mother was not pretty anymore, but the ghost of someone pretty. Small brown spots lurked underneath Delia's cheeks as though her skin were a threadbare rug, outlasting its usefulness.

Babe sat down next to Delia. She dusted off the few things she'd collected. She felt like just one more object, stranded in this ruined world.

A gentle wind moved around them. Babe watched as the cinders blew away like feathers, making the ground beneath them visible, revealing a hoofprint in the blackened dirt. When she looked further, she saw the wide, dark trail cut by the frightened herd, the first surviving memory, embedded in the earth.

TWO CRIMINALS

This is not my first crime. The first I committed twenty years ago. The crime then, as now: impersonating Joe, my younger, myopic brother who could not pass the DMV eye exam without the aid of his tumbler-thick glasses. I had perfect eyesight back then. I took the test for him.

In our opinions the crime was blameless. Who, after all, could be expected to live in the San Fernando Valley and *not* drive a car? The fact that Joe was burdened with these imperfect eyes on top of all his other impediments was the real crime. As far as we were concerned, we were heroes, rogue cowboys in our own Wild West of strip malls, movie theaters, and orange groves (for there were still orange groves in the Valley then, sweet-stinking and fly-ridden.) We were evening the score.

It was a simple crime, really. First, Joe took a moment to scan the driving manual in the parking lot. Then he sauntered inside the low cinder-block building and effortlessly sailed through his written test. Next, he performed an imitation of himself having an asthma attack which was so authentic that those around him in that crowded, sticky room became stricken with alarm and their own reluctance to help. Joe had seen those pitying, uncomfortable thank-God-he's-not-my-kid stares before. He had made the instantaneous transition from one of us to one of them a thousand times. But now the rejection worked in his favor. He mumbled something about lifelong asthma and inhalers and left the building.

Outside, I waited in the scorched mid-August parking lot. The harsh Valley sun slammed down on my head, then careened off the shiny pelts of the parked cars. I watched people hurry in and out of the building, holding purses and rolled-up newspapers over their brows to shield their eyes from the glare. I was nervous. Being the only person fool enough to stand in the middle of a steaming parking lot seemed to me irrefutable evidence of our guilt.

Joe came out of the DMV clutching his chest so realistically that I began to reach for the fat medicine kit we kept stashed under the front seat of the car. But then he dropped his hands and smiled. His narrow face and dark eyes lit up with the pleasure of our deceit.

"I'm a genius," he said when he reached the car. He handed me his wallet and with it his identity. "All right, son," he said somberly. "Do our family proud."

I pocketed the wallet. We looked enough alike that we

could be casually mistaken for one another if a person did not know us well. In my identical green T-shirt and jeans, I walked inside the DMV, consciously imitating Joe's nonchalant shuffle, the way his toes never left the ground when he walked. I found the eye exam line and took my place at its end, avoiding any curious gazes. I focused, instead, on the woman ahead of me whose flesh poured from beneath her workout bra in pancake-batter folds of fat. As I imagined lying in that pool of flesh as buoyant as tapioca pudding, I felt my groin tighten. But when the woman shifted her weight, revealing lines of sweat trapped in the creases of her back, the fantasy took a nose-dive. Everybody in the room was half dressed—in shorts, netted tank shirts, sundresses creeping high up the thigh. It was summer in the Valley and dressing was an afterthought. You'd see people in bathing suits pumping gas into their cars, or in pajamas picking up a quart of milk at the 7-Eleven.

The pancake-batter lady was at the counter now, covering her left eye with a long black spoon. My stomach roiled nervously. Suddenly, in a moment where our similarity was vital, I was struck with how unlike my brother I was. My body was bulky with braided muscles—an athlete's physique which I'd worked hard to achieve between and sometimes at the expense of classes. At night, I'd lift weights on the floor of our shared bedroom while Joe lay above me on his bed, making plans for us to go to Amsterdam and smoke pot all day. Standing in the examination line, I willed my chest to cave in, my back to hunch slightly, for twenty pounds to miraculously fall away so my body would become Joe's. But it was useless. After a lifetime of shouldering my brother's infirmities, it was no more possible to shed my good health than for him to don it. We were brothers in all things, but our bodies were our great divide.

When I reached the front of the line, I handed over Joe's application and identification, and discreetly coughed into my hands—an uncanny imitation learned from years of listening to Joe's asthmatic wheezes. I looked away as the examiner floated his gaze over the picture. When I dared to look back, he had pulled the collar of his shirt out and was blowing down towards his sweaty chest in a feeble attempt to cool himself off.

"Go," he instructed, looking up past me to judge the line.

Quickly, I put the spoon to my left eye and read the diminishing letters on the eye chart, my heart fluttering double-time.

"Stop," the man said, like a talking traffic light.

In that silence between my last *s, z, p* and whatever hell might follow, I had an almost uncontrollable urge to foul the whole thing up, to make some embarrassing sound, maybe moo.

Joe would never have lost his composure. He worked the angles of his life like an expert con man, playing on everyone's expectations. He could take a few short breaths, rest unsteadily on a desk, and a teacher would up a grade from a C to a B. Girls melted in his waifish presence, and he was the recipient of all their mixed-up maternal sexuality.

"Go," the man repeated, sliding a paper across the counter to me. I was confused. *Go where? Go again?* But then I realized it was *go away* and that we'd done it. Joe and I had committed a perfect crime.

Outside, I waved the flag: Joe's temporary license, his freedom. My celebration died, however, when I saw him suck on his inhaler for real this time. Stress always brought on the asthma. That and the general decrepitude of the air in Los Angeles. On hot days like these, when soot stuck to the sky like a permanent bathtub ring and parents kept their children inside, breath became Joe's enemy.

When I reached the car, he held up a hand and took one more blast of his inhaler.

"How'd it go?" he asked, his eyes watery from the spasm. "Did they buy it?"

"I should be a goddamn movie star," I answered, slapping the license down on the hood of the Datsun. "They should give me an Academy Award."

"Not likely," Joe said, tucking his inhaler into his jeans pocket. "You're too ugly."

"At least I can breathe."

"Philip scores with his incredibly subtle sense of humor," Joe cried out in an announcer's voice. "And the crowd goes wild. Yaaaa!"

This new crime is something else altogether.

Joe and I are alone in his hospital room. It is two in the afternoon, twenty years later. He's dying.

I have taught my last history class of the day at the same high school Joe and I attended as kids. Now I can spend the afternoon with my brother until visiting hours are over. It's funny how much I enjoy coming to this cold place, not simply because I can spend what time remains with Joe, but because it keeps me from going home to my orderly house, my desk full of papers to grade, the fact of my survival. I live alone not far from where Joe and I grew up. I've come close to getting married, but I backed away from it. I don't want children. I don't think I have it in me to take care of anybody else.

Joe is hooked up to an I.V. and oxygen stands at the ready should he need it. His normally narrow face is thinner. His eyes are sunken and rimmed with gray, his lips are dry and cracked as the desert floor. I take some ice from a plastic cup at his bedside and rub it over his mouth, which glistens for a moment before the moisture is sucked in by his thirsty pores. We've been sitting together for half an hour. He has drifted off to sleep. I'm counting his breaths.

"I want us to talk," I tell him when he finally wakes. "I want you to listen to me."

He opens his eyes halfway. "And here I was going to suggest a set of tennis," he replies softly.

"What I want to say," I continue, then stop. I take off my glasses and rub my eyes. "This is hard."

"*This* is hard," he says, gesturing to his useless body. "Dying is hard."

"Sorry. I didn't mean—"

Joe stops me with the barest trace of his old wicked smile. "I love doing that," he says hoarsely. "I get to be so evil now that I'm almost dead."

"You're still a jerk."

"It's like those drug-resistant bacteria," he says, sucking in a rattling breath. "My acid wit will live millions of years after we're all dead and gone."

My eyes well up. I'm so relieved to see a glimmer of the old Joe. "Listen," I say, again. "I want to talk about the possibility of the adoption not happening. . . . "

"Not happening in time, you mean."

"Yeah. It's just something to think about. The possibility, I mean."

Joe is quiet. He stares up at the television, which dangles from the ceiling like a loose tooth. Then his body stiffens as if he's beginning to seize.

"The girls are *mine*," he says, bringing down one fist with such force that he inadvertently presses the button by his bony hand and half the bed begins to levitate. The I.V. tube threatens to become tangled up in the guardrail. Joe looks to me and I move swiftly in the dance of rescue that has defined our life together. I do not let baby Joe fall down. I do not let little Joe run too fast at school. I fight his bullies, monitor the medications, save his life in a hundred mundane ways.

I press the button. The headrest begins its patient journey back down. "We should get the nurse to unplug this thing," I say, waving the bed-control device. "They don't know how dangerous you are with heavy equipment."

Joe stares at the ceiling, ignoring my joke. "The girls are mine," he says softly.

Actually, he's wrong. The daughters he's raised for the last ten years are not really his at all. Officially, they belong to Jenna and her first husband. They were teenagers when they met and had two babies by the time they were twenty. They lived in a shack in the hills above Cabrillo beach. He was a carpenter and one day, he didn't come home from a job. He

left no note, or half-hearted excuse, or even, Jenna often says
with a shake of her nose ring and her soft brown curls, a
decent lie.

Joe raised Hazel and Anna as his own from the time he met
Jenna, when the girls were three and five. He'd taken to sudden fatherhood willingly and young—he was only twenty-six.
While our friends scoffed at marriage as though it was a
prison only a fool would walk into, Joe knew he had better get
started sooner than later.

For years it had never seemed important for Joe to adopt
Hazel and Anna. The idea was almost repugnant to him, as if
simply loving them wasn't enough. But now, as he is about to
die, it matters to Joe that they are his and that the world
knows it.

"They love you like a father," I say. "Your *are* their father."

"But he could come back," Joe says weakly. "Like a ghost or
some horrible late-night movie monster."

"The Return of the Evil . . . Dad!" I say, my voice trembling
with ersatz drama. In better days Joe would riff on this, sum-
moning up the backlog of wretched movies that occupied far
too much of our youth. He would remember everything,
every actor, every detail of story, his mind an elegant storage
bin of the disposable culture that obsessed us.

To my relief, Joe laughs. But the laugh turns into a sputter
of coughs and desperate gasps.

"Okay. Okay," I whisper. I reach for the call button.

"No," he says, waving it away. We wait for a few minutes as
his breath evens out.

"The idea of this guy coming out of nowhere to claim

Anna and Hazel is much worse than the idea of dying," Joe says finally. "Which isn't really an idea anymore. It's more like a thing, sitting here. Like one of Anna's pimples."

Inadvertently, I touch the little rivulets that crisscross my cheeks, mementos of my own youthful battle with acne which made me shy despite my athletic prowess. I never had luck socially, but, keeping an eye on Joe all the time, I never felt lonely. The scars are less obvious now, as they are intermingled with the creases brought on by sun and age.

"How many more days does Evil Dad have?" Joe asks.

"Twenty."

We are both quiet, silently weighing this amount of time against Joe's rapidly failing body.

"Twenty days," he muses, his gaze wandering off into the chalk-white corner of the room.

It is five o'clock. Jenna and the girls burst into the room, sudden and colorful, like a bouquet of flowers popping out of a magician's hat. The perfumes of Hazel's post–soccer game sweat, Anna's patchouli oil (that first, overzealous scent of adolescence), and the indeterminate spicy smell that is synonymous with Jenna mix to form a magnetic odor.

"Dad!" Hazel calls out happily, parking herself on the bed next to Joe's legs. The dirt of her soccer socks rubs off on the clean hospital sheets. "We won. I scored twice!"

She reaches around and grabs her hair tie to let loose her scraggly red mane, then wipes her nose with her forearm. At thirteen, Hazel is caught between the boy/girl she wants to remain and the woman she is inexorably becoming. She'll still

plop down on Joe's lap and lean her body up against his, warm
and puppyish. But then he'll catch her studying herself in the
hallway mirror, her hand running down her chest to gauge her
new geography.

Slowly, Joe lifts his hand to dole out the customary high
five. Hazel is careful not to put too much muscle into her slap.
I recognize her athlete's sense of superiority. Her body glides
as if every joint and hinge were well oiled; she seems to take
pleasure in movement itself. She is a happy girl, blessed with
the gift of being unobservant. Her awareness of the world is
not wide enough to take in what might trouble her.

Her sister, Anna, stands back, judging Joe's status. At fifteen,
she is wary and complicated, harder to love. She's a cautious
girl who measures anything she says or does against all other
possible options.

"Anna," Joe says, reaching out for her.

She ventures close to him, lays her long, delicate fingers in
his, but keeps her arm straight, putting distance between her
father and herself. Her eyes sweep the room, taking in everything, resting for an extra beat on the respirator, the newest
member of Joe's mechanical staff. Her expression registers
nothing, but I know she is filing away this piece of information, judging its ripple effect on her future.

"What's up?" Joe says, smiling broadly. It is a heartbreaking
gesture which seems to require the engagement of every muscle in his face.

"Not much," she answers as her eyes shift away from him.
"What's this for?" She lifts her chin in the direction of the respirator.

"Oxygen," he says. "In case I need a little help."

"Do you need it?"

"Sometimes."

"Sometimes," she repeats. "What does that mean?"

"It means that things are getting harder."

"Okay," she says, nodding. "I understand."

"Understand what?" Hazel says. Worry spreads over her soft cheeks like a suddenly appearing rain cloud.

"Girls," Jenna interrupts. "Let's eat in the cafeteria tonight. I don't have anything at home." She puts her hand gently on Hazel's back. Jenna's flowery dress falls slightly off one shoulder, revealing the tip of one of her tattoos.

"Can we eat now? I'm starving," Hazel announces.

"You two go down and I'll meet you there. I just want to talk to Uncle Philip for a second," Jenna says. "Okay, Anna?"

Anna looks pained by the idea. I imagine how hard it is for her to be in this place. She must see so much, not just the sickness, but the quiet dread of relatives, and the busy gait of doctors and nurses who know more than they will say.

"I'm not hungry," she says.

But Jenna reaches into her purse and hands Anna a ten-dollar bill. "I'll be right there," she says calmly.

Hazel gives Joe a quick kiss and hops off the bed. Head bowed, Anna follows her sister out. When the heavy door closes behind them, Jenna gives Joe a full, lustful kiss.

"You take my breath away," Joe says. "Literally."

"I'm beat," she announces energetically. "I just got needled and I'm fried. It can be exhausting to get rid of all that blocked chi."

"I loved your blocked chi," Joe says. "How could you get rid of it without asking me first?"

They laugh and I marvel once again at the fact that Joe ended up with Jenna. She talks about the spirit like it's a kindly neighbor you might run into at the grocery store. She eagerly embraces whatever is alternative and unscientific. She's been channeled, visualized, rolfed, and aromatherapied. She's hennaed her hair and her hands, shaved her head in order to free herself of vanity, grown dreadlocks to accomplish the same goal. Cynicism makes her sad. She listens to Joe's sharp-edged jokes with a perplexed expression on her face, as though she does not understand what language he is speaking, but is too polite to mention it. For Joe's part, he rolls his eyes when she doses him with magical-sounding herbs, never believing for a minute that she can cure him. But it turns out he loves it all— her potions and her faith that there is something else going on while we go about what we mistakenly consider our lives.

I am grateful to her. Maybe this is because she has assumed my burden, taking over the watchman's job I performed throughout my youth. But more than this, I am grateful that she has never given Joe reason to doubt her. Her love is uncomplicated and unpitying. She loves him the way you might love a sweet, ripe peach: it's a plain love, the same every time out.

Now she smiles and Joe relaxes for the first time all day. Her smile is a balm to him, a quiet, peaceful lake. I hope that, when he goes, her smile will be the last thing he sees.

"I have a bit of news," she says, a flicker of tension immobilizing her face. "I got a call. From Rick."

The silence in the room is worse than death. Or maybe this is what death feels like: the opposite of everything. Rick is Jenna's ex-husband and the girls' real father. Joe lets out a small, sharp wail.

Adoption has proven to be a tediously long process. A year ago, when Joe was still reasonably healthy, he filed the papers. Months passed before a hearing was set to determine cause. There, he pleaded passionately and convincingly for the girls and they, in turn, took the stand and asked that Joe be made their legal father. Jenna and I sat on the sidelines, trying not to cry.

Anna spoke first, enumerating with a scientist's accuracy the reasons why Joe should be made her real father. "He takes good care of us," she said quietly. "He provides food and clothing and our home. He does our homework with us. He gets angry when we mess up, which I think is right for a father to do."

Then it was Hazel's turn. She was agitated on the stand. She wore a dress, which was unusual for her, and she could not find a comfortable way to sit in it. She twisted and retwisted her legs, then the ends of her braid; at one point she even pulled a strand of hair through the gap between her two front teeth. Her words were scattered and halting as she tried to answer the questions put to her. Finally she became exasperated. "He's my dad," she blurted out. "I don't know what else you want me to say." It was like a line of music untroubled by trills. Even the judge had to agree. The adoption was incontestable.

Except it wasn't. Months followed while papers were shifted from one agency desk to another. Then we waited while "all best efforts" were made to locate this phantom father. Phone calls were placed to long-since-disconnected numbers, relatives were sought who either turned up dead or had no more idea of Rick's whereabouts than we did. By then, Joe's condition had declined rapidly and he was in and out of the hospital. The adoption was no longer a legal procedure. It was a race.

I'm the first to break the silence in the hospital room. "How did they find him?"

"They found his sister and she found him. In Chicago," Jenna says evenly, trying to maintain her composure. "He's coming tomorrow."

"No," Joe says and begins to shake his head violently from side to side.

Jenna leans forward and places her hands on either side of his face in order to stop him. "Shhh," she whispers. "It's okay."

"He can't see the girls," Joe says.

"He didn't say anything about the girls," Jenna says. "He asked to meet you."

"Why should Joe have to meet him?" I say angrily. "Tell him to call your lawyer. Joe shouldn't be involved in this at all."

Jenna responds carefully, "I get the feeling that bringing a lawyer into all this might make things worse. We don't know what Rick wants yet."

"He's getting on an airplane. He wants something," I say. "He has no right to the girls."

"No court!" Joe shouts. "I don't want the girls in court. I don't want them to go through that again."

"I feel that if we make it about lawyers, Rick will too," Jenna responds evenly. She looks down at Joe. "When he meets you, he'll know you should be their father. He'll feel the rightness of it."

"So we're talking karma now, is that it?" I say.

Jenna ignores my insult.

"And when he sees me?" Joe asks, gesturing to his frail body. "I'm sure he'll think a cadaver's the perfect father for his daughters."

Jenna lifts her hands to her eyes. "We don't know what he'll do," she says weakly. "Maybe he grew up," she adds. "It's been thirteen years."

"He abandoned his wife and kids without a word," Joe says. "I don't think you grow out of that kind of flaw."

"He's already on his way and we can't stop him," she answers, beginning to cry. Joe reaches out for her and she sits beside him, laying her head on his chest. He weaves his fingers through her tangle of hair.

"Fuck this shit," he says quietly, without rancor. "You know how we always tell the girls not to curse?"

Jenna's head bobs up and down.

"We were wrong," he continues. "Sometimes *shit* and *fuck* are the goddamn best words in the English language. Tell the girls that, will you?"

Jenna lifts her head and smiles. Exhausted, I slump in the chair next to the wall.

"Well, the answer is obvious," Joe says finally.

"I'll call the lawyer," I say, anticipating him.

"Philip will have to pretend to be me," Joe continues.

"It's not a game," I say wearily.

"Yes it is," he says, looking at me. "That's exactly what it is. You go and meet him. He'll never know the difference."

"Joe," Jenna says. "Come on."

"And what am I supposed to do when I meet him?" I say, "Beat him up?"

"You'll convince him," Joe says.

"This is not you doing my homework for me," I say gently. "This won't work."

"This *will* work," Joe says, galvanized. A light has returned to his eyes and I half expect him to leap out of his bed.

"How about if you're wrong?" I continue. "What if he drags us to court anyway? I'm sure this is some kind of crime. Fraud or impersonation. They don't surrender custody to criminals, last time I checked."

Joe erupts. "He is not getting my girls!"

His explosion dissolves into a spasm. Jenna dives for the call button. Immediately, two nurses invade the room like a SWAT team, pushing us aside. Jenna and I huddle in the corner.

"Out! Now!" one of them barks back over her shoulder.

Jenna and I slink out into the corridor, where we lean against the railing which runs down the center of the mauve and tan wall. Jenna slides to the floor, tucking her dress into the backs of her knees. I crouch down next to her.

"Maybe," Jenna says, "when you get this close to dying, everything in your life gets so terrible that the next place can only be a relief." She glances at me. "I know you're secretly rolling your eyes right now, Philip."

"No," I say, caught. "Well, yeah. A little, maybe."

"I want to kill Rick," she says suddenly. I'm so surprised that I laugh. Jenna giggles and covers her mouth. "I do," she continues giddily. "I want to rip him apart for what he's doing to Joe."

"Bravo," I say, clapping my hands. "Some old-fashioned ungenerous thoughts."

Our laughter dies down and we're quiet again.

"I'd do what he's asking if I thought it would work," I say finally.

She reaches for my hand. "I know you would," she says, squeezing my fingers tight.

"It's just like him. Scheming up to the very last."

"It's reassuring, isn't it?" she muses.

"I guess."

"We need that, don't we?" she continues. "He's the one who's dying, but we need *him* to reassure *us*."

"Why is that?"

"I don't know," she says sadly. "I miss him already."

Jenna has arranged for me to meet Rick at a restaurant on the beach. I know the place. You can eat halfway decent shrimp and crab and they give you a bucket of free peanuts to keep you drinking. The emptied shells carpet the ground. The room smells of sweet, sticky old beer and briny fish.

I arrive fifteen minutes early. In order to pull this off, I have to be the one in control. If Rick catches me off guard, I'll surely make a mistake. I've stopped at the cash machine on the way so that I won't have to pull out a credit card. I haven't figured out any other way for him to catch on unless someone I know sees me. But this is unlikely. My life still occupies the same square miles of my youth. No one I know would drive all the way out to the beach on a weekday for mediocre fish and a beer.

Many men walk in and out. In my hasty conversation with Jenna, I forgot to ask her what her ex-husband looks like. This mistake makes the arrangement seem like folly from the outset. I consider leaving, but then a man walks in. He stops at the door, as if he is deciding whether or not to enter. His hands are jammed down into his blue jeans pockets, causing his back to hunch and his shoulders to rise up around his ears. I recognize the discomfort. It must be Rick. He's not the fighter I imagined confronting. He is short and heavy around the middle. I stand up at my table and wave. The gesture seems feeble, like I am trying to flag down a waiter who refuses to look my way.

Rick walks slowly over to the table and stands behind a chair. "Rick Fiore," he says, pulling his hand out of his pocket and shaking mine.

"Joe," I say. "I'm Joe."

There's an awkward moment until I begin to sit and gesture toward the empty chair. He pulls it out and sits too. He looks down, fingering his cocktail napkin. His hands are like paws; the stubby nails are beside the point on his massive fingers. His leather jacket is worn thin and the wrist bands are frayed.

Neither of us says anything for a long time, as though we are in a contest to see who will crack first.

"How was your trip?" I ask finally, unable to bear the quiet any longer.

"Fine. I don't fly much."

We retreat into silence once more.

"You've lived in Chicago a long time?" I ask.

"Upwards of ten years."

He looks away in order to avoid me. I know he means thirteen years. The same thirteen he's been absent from his daughters' lives. I've scored a point and start to feel better. Joe would be proud.

"I was in Chicago for a conference once," I say. "It's a good city. Lots to do."

"Ummm," he says, uneasy with my small talk.

"You still work construction?"

He nods.

"Housing starts are up," I say. "That ought to be good news for you." Money rolling in and none of it going to your daughters. I'm beginning to enjoy myself.

"I spoke to a lawyer," he says, abruptly. "I have rights. I don't have to sign those papers just because I haven't been in the picture."

I'm about to challenge him, but I hold my tongue. Joe wants no lawyers. He doesn't want the girls in court.

"What I've been thinking," he says, "is that I did the wrong thing by those girls. And now, if I just let some judge take me off those papers like I never existed . . . " He shakes his head. "The way I see it, that would be worse. I have to take responsibility."

"You haven't taken any for thirteen years. Suddenly you're going to start now?"

"People make mistakes," he says, glaring at me.

"So this is about your guilt," I say. "Not about what's right for the girls. Or what's right for my family," I add. The words feel like heavy coins in my mouth.

"Sure it's about my guilt. Sure it is," he says.

His frankness unnerves me.

"You know," he continues, "I think about what I did all the time. I mean, the girls are probably better off the way things worked out. But I'm no monster. If I take my name off those papers, it's like I'm erasing who they are."

"You're not who they are. They don't even know you. I'm who they are. I am." I'm practically yelling across the table but the words sound hollow.

"I'm saying if someday they want to meet me, or talk to me, or yell at me, I think they should be able to."

"You're not going to sign the papers, are you?" I ask.

"Not without a fight."

"You'll lose."

"I'll get what I want," he says calmly. "They'll know I tried."

I rub my face with my hands. I'm a history teacher. I look for the truth in the lies and reconstructions of memory. Here's a reasonable man making a wildly illogical argument. Or maybe it's the other way around. I can't tell anymore. I don't know what the right thing to do is. What I do know is that to even ask the question is to fail my brother.

"Do you want to see the girls?" I say before I'm even aware of it.

Rick looks at me, startled, than narrows his gaze as he tries to figure out why I've offered him this prize.

"What do you mean?" he says, leaning forward.

As he does, something in the air between us shifts. I've changed the rules and he's nervous.

"See the girls. Right now. Yes or no?" I demand.

"Sure," he says hesitantly. "I guess that'd be something."

Hazel plays soccer on Tuesdays and Thursdays in Van Nuys, a bear of a drive from the beach. It will take us forty-five minutes in traffic if we're lucky. In my rearview mirror, I see Rick's rented car following me, lane change for lane change, as we travel east on the Coast Highway. The late afternoon sun glints off the water. A couple of brave souls are surfing. Someone manipulates a Geiger counter across the sand. When the highway veers away from the beach, we head onto the San Diego Freeway and towards the Valley. I regret my suggestion more with each passing mile. I feel like a guide leading some weekend hunter to his prey, positioning him so perfectly that there's no way he could miss making the kill. I don't know how I'll explain this to Joe and Jenna. I try to distract myself with the radio, but the late afternoon chatter filled with traffic alerts and sexual innuendo makes me tense. I check my mirror. Rick is still on my tail.

Once off the freeway, we drive through Van Nuys. There are still buildings boarded up from the big earthquake a few years ago. Whole blocks are nothing more than the shells of construction, making it impossible to tell if buildings are being put up or torn down. The corners boast mini-malls with Mexican fast-food joints, gas stations, maybe a dentist's office or a check-cashing store. Kids with pants as baggy as potato sacks practice skateboard tricks on the smooth surface of driveways.

The park is a vast landfill bordered on one side by the Hollywood Freeway. On the other side runs the L.A. River, which looks more like a slow-draining bathtub than any useful waterway. Rick and I pull our cars onto a blacktop a good distance from the soccer field where a pack of uniformed girls are sprinkled over the grass, rushing back and forth chasing a ball. Anna will be there too, sitting on the side, her nose in a book, waiting for Hazel to finish and for one of the mothers to drive them home, giving Jenna more time at the hospital.

We get out of our cars. Rick looks at me uncomfortably. "I was thinking of losing you back there," he says. "Around Sepulveda."

I nod. It is impossible not to acknowledge that we'd both rather be anywhere else but here.

"I don't know about this," he says, as if he's read my own ambivalence. He shoves his hands into his pockets, as if binding them to his body might prevent him from making another disastrous choice. He drags his foot along the pavement of the parking lot, tracing some incomprehensible design in the thin layer of sand and dirt. Maybe someone will see his S.O.S. and untangle us from this mess we've made.

"I see the girls," I say, staring off across the field at the dots of white and red.

"Yeah?" he says, looking up.

"Hazel is number eight. Her team has the red jerseys. Anna, she'll be the one reading. She has long brown hair. She looks like . . . " I stop short because I am about to say she looks like him. I am stunned by the accuracy of this realization. Her dark gaze and her careful, judicious manner are his. "She's a serious girl," I say instead.

Rick looks out across the field as if he has been asked to walk into a wall of fire. "I want to know something," he says.

My stomach flips over. "What?" I ask, ready to come clean.

"I want to know what being their father is like," he says.

My adrenaline is pumping so strongly that I almost don't hear him. "What?" I repeat dumbly.

"What's it like?"

"The girls?" I say, scrambling to pull myself together. "Well, Anna's smart as anything. She's top of her class. She's a real thinker. She's—"

"No." Rick cuts me off. "I don't mean what are they like. I mean what is it like to be their dad?"

I try to imagine Joe's life. He must kiss his girls good morning and drive them to school. He might check over their homework at the end of the day, but maybe they're too old for that. But what do they say to one another when they pass in the hallway, or while brushing their teeth in the bathroom, or during those slow miles in the car? What does he feel when he comes upon them with their heads bowed towards cereal bowls, when they don't realize he's there?

"Well," I start carefully. "I guess it makes you see things differently."

He nods and leans his body forward, soaking up every word I'm saying. His eagerness makes my fraudulence nearly unbearable.

"I don't know how to answer your question," I say finally.

Rick waves me off. "It's idiotic, right?" he says, smiling for the first time since we've met. "You can only know your own life, right? Not the ones you didn't live." He looks back to the soccer game. "It's okay? A guy just hanging around, watching the game?" he asks. "They're not going to call the cops on me or anything?"

"It's a public park."

"I wish I had a dog or something." We both laugh.

He hunches his shoulders and starts towards the game. After about twenty yards, he stops. He's no closer to the girls than he was a month, or a year, ago. He stands there for what feels like minutes, still as a statue. Then he turns and walks off the field, gets into his car, and drives off.

The girls finish their practice. They jump up and down, fall into awkward clumps of hugs and high fives. Where is the hand for me to slap?

On the way back home, I drive along Ventura Boulevard. It's much more built up than it was when Joe and I were kids. I pass three different bagel chains and grocery stores built like palaces. It looks more exciting now, but for all the activity, not much more is really going on.

A soft twilight has replaced the sun. The lamps along the boulevard glow faintly. Neon on the storefronts begins to stand out against the growing darkness. A few people walk, but mostly the sidewalk is empty; the life of the boulevard is inside the cars now. The colors of the sky begin to make themselves felt. It was a smoggy day; it will be a brilliant sunset.

WHAT I SAW FROM WHERE I STOOD

Dulcie is afraid of freeways. She doesn't like not being able to get off whenever she wants, and sometimes I catch her holding her breath between exits, as if she's driving past a graveyard. So, even though the party we went to last week was miles from our apartment in Silver Lake, we drove home on the surface streets.

I was drunk, and Dulcie was driving my car. She'd taken one look at me as we left the party, then dug her fingers into my pants pocket and pulled out my keys. I liked the feel of her hand rubbing against me through my jeans; she hadn't been touching me much lately.

I cranked open the window to clear my head as we drove through Santa Monica. Nice houses. Pretty flowers. Volvos.

Dulcie and I always say we'd never want to live out here in suburbia, but the truth is, we can't afford to, not on our salaries. Dulcie's a second-grade teacher in Glendale, and I'm a repairman for the telephone company.

When we reached Hollywood, things got livelier. There were skinny guitar punks patrolling the clubs on the strip with their pudgy girlfriends in midriff tops and thigh-high black skirts. A lot of big hair, big breasts, boredom. Farther east, there were boys strutting the boulevard, waiting to slip into some-one's silver Mercedes and make a buck. One leaned against a fire hydrant and picked at his sallow face, looking cold in a muscle T-shirt.

We hit a red light at Vermont, right next to the hospital where Dulcie lost the baby, a year ago. She'd started cramping badly one night. She was only six months pregnant. I called the emergency room, and the attendant said to come right over. By the time we got there, the doctors couldn't pick up a heartbeat. They gave Dulcie drugs to induce labor and the baby was born. He was blue. He was no bigger than a football.

Dulcie looked up at the hospital and then back at the road. She's a small girl and she sank behind the wheel, getting even smaller. I didn't say anything. The light turned green. She drove across Vermont and I nodded off.

I woke up when a car plowed into us from behind. My body flew towards the windshield, then ricocheted back against my seat. Dulcie gripped the wheel, staring straight ahead out the windshield.

"Something happened," she said.

"Yeah," I heard myself answer, although my voice sounded hollow. "We had an accident."

We got out to check the damage and met at the back of the car. "It's nothing," Dulcie said, as we studied the medium-sized dent on the fender. It was nothing to us, anyway; the car was too old and beat-up for us to feel protective of it.

Behind me, I heard the door of a van slide open. I hadn't thought about the people who'd hit us, hadn't even noticed if they bothered to stop. I started to wave them off. They didn't need to get out, apologize, dig around for the insurance information they probably didn't have. But when I turned around, there were four or five men in front of me. They were standing very close. They were young. I was beginning to think that Dulcie and I should just get back into our car and drive away, when the van's engine cut out and a tall guy wearing a hooded sweatshirt called back towards it. "Yo, Darren! Turn it on, you motherfucker!"

His cursing seemed to make his friends nervous. Two of them looked at their feet. One hopped up and down like a fighter getting ready for a bout. Someone was saying "Shit, shit, shit" over and over again. Then I heard "Do it, do it!" and a short, wide kid with a shaved head and glow-in-the-dark stripes on his sneakers pulled out a gun and pointed it at my face. It didn't look like the guns in movies. Dulcie screamed.

"Don't shoot. Please don't shoot us!" Her voice was so high it sounded painful, as if it were scraping her throat.

"Your keys!" the tall one shouted. "Give us your mother-fucking keys!"

Dulcie threw the keys on the ground at their feet. "Please! I don't have any money!"

"I'll get it," I heard myself say, as if I were picking up the tab at a bar. I was calm. I felt like I was underwater. Everything seemed slow and all I could hear was my own breathing. I reached into my back pocket and pulled out my wallet. I took out the bills and handed them over. The tall guy grabbed the money and ran back to the van, which made me feel better until I noticed that the kid with the shaved head was still pointing the gun at me.

That's when I got scared. As though someone had thrown a switch, all the sound returned, loud and close. I heard the cars roaring past on Sunset. I heard Dulcie screaming "No! No! No!" I heard an argument erupt between two of the guys. "Get in their car! Get in their fucking car or I'll do you too!" I grabbed Dulcie's hand, and I pulled her around the front of our car, crouching low. I could feel the heat of the engine under the hood. The van revved up. I stood, bringing Dulcie up with me, and there, on the driver's side, no more than three feet away, was the kid with the shaved head. He had the gun in one hand and Dulcie's keys in the other. I could see sweat glistening over the pimples on his face.

"Hey!" he said, looking confused. "What the fuck?"

Then it was as if I skipped a few minutes of my life, because the next thing I knew, Dulcie and I were racing down a side street toward the porch lights of some bungalows. We didn't look back to see if we were being followed. Sometimes Dulcie held my hand, sometimes we were separated by the row of parked cars. We had no idea where we were going.

After the police and their questions, and their heartfelt assurance that there was nothing at all they could do for us, we took a cab back to our apartment in Silver Lake. Dulcie was worried because the crack heads—that's what the police called them—had our keys, and our address was on the car registration. But the police had told us that the carjackers wouldn't come after us—that kind of thing almost never happened.

Still, Dulcie couldn't sleep, so we sat up all night while she went over what had happened. She'd seen the van on the street earlier, but hadn't it been in front of us, not behind? Why had they chosen our car, our sorry, broken-down mutt of a car? How close had we come to being shot?

"We saw them," she said. "We know what they look like."

"They weren't killers. They were thieves. There's a difference, I guess," I said.

"No," she said, twisting her straight brown hair around her finger so tightly the tip turned white. "It doesn't make sense."

Dulcie needs things to be exact. You have to explain yourself clearly when you're around her, so she's probably a good teacher. For a minute I wondered whether she wished we had been shot, just for the sake of logic.

She'd done this after losing the baby, too, going over and over what she might have done to kill it. Had she exercised too much? Not enough? Had she eaten something bad? She wanted an answer, and she needed to blame someone; if that person turned out to be her, that would still be better than having no one to blame at all. A few days after the delivery, a hospital social worker called to check on her. She reassured

Dulcie that what had happened hadn't been her fault. It was a fluke thing, the woman said. She used the word *flukish*.

"I should have noticed them tailing me," Dulcie said now. "How could I not notice a car that close?"

"Don't do that," I told her. "Don't think about what could have happened."

"I have to think about it," she said. "How can you not think about it? We were this close," she said, holding her fingers out like a gun and aiming at my chest.

I drove Dulcie's car to work the next day. When I got home that night, Dulcie had moved our mattress from our bed into the living room, where it lay in the middle of the floor, the sheets spilling over onto the carpet. She'd taken a personal day to recover from the holdup. Her eyes were red, and she looked as though she'd been crying all afternoon.

"It's the rat," she said. "He's back."

A month earlier, a rat had burrowed and nested in the wall behind our bed. Every night, it scratched a weird, personal jazz into our ears. We told the landlord and he said he would get on it right away, which meant: You'll be living with that rat forever, and if you don't like it there're ten other people in line for your apartment. I checked around the house to make sure the rat couldn't find a way inside. I patched up a hole underneath the sink with plywood and barricaded the space between the dishwasher and the wall with old towels. After Dulcie was sure that there would be no midnight visitor eating our bananas, she was okay with the rat. We even named him—Mingus.

She wasn't okay with it anymore.

"He's getting louder. Closer. Like he's going to get in this time," she said.

"He can't get in. There's no way."

"Well, I can't sleep in that room."

"It's a small apartment, Dulcie." The living room was smaller than the bedroom, and the mattress nearly filled it.

"I can't do it, Charles. I can't."

"All right. We can sleep anywhere you want," I said.

"I want to sleep in the living room. And I want you to change the message on the answering machine," she said. "It has my voice on it. It should have a man's voice."

"You're worried about the rat hearing your voice on the machine?"

"Don't make fun of me, okay? Those guys know where we live."

Later that night, I discovered that she wanted to sleep with all the lights on.

"I want people to know we're home," she said. "People don't break in if they think you're there."

We were lying on the floor on our mattress. She felt tiny, so delicate that I would crush her if I squeezed too hard or rolled the wrong way.

"You don't mind, do you?" she said. "About the light. Is it too bright?"

She'd let me throw one of my shirts, an orange one, over the fixture hanging from the ceiling. It gave the room a muf-fled, glowy feel.

"No," I said. I kissed her forehead. She didn't turn to me. Since the baby, we've had a hard time getting together.

Dulcie sat up again. "Maybe it's a bad idea," she said. "Maybe a thief will see the light on at four A.M. and think that we're actually out of town. I mean, who leaves their light on all night when they're home?"

"No one."

"You know," she said, "I saw in a catalogue once that you could buy an inflatable man to put in a chair by your window. Or in your car. You could put him in the passenger seat if you were driving alone."

She looked at me, but I didn't know what to say. To me, driving with a plastic blow-up doll in the seat next to you seemed very peculiar.

"Lie down," I said, stroking her back beneath her T-shirt. Her skin was smooth and warm.

She lay down next to me. I turned over on my stomach and laid my hand across her chest. I liked the feel of the small rises of her breasts, the give of them.

Dulcie's milk had come in two days after the delivery. The doctor had warned her that this would happen and had pre-scribed Valium in advance. I came home from work and found Dulcie, stoned, staring at her engorged breasts in the bathroom mirror. I'd never seen anything like it. Her breasts were like boulders, and her veins spread out across them like waterways on a map. Dulcie squeezed one nipple, and a little pearl of yel-lowish milk appeared. She tasted it.

"It's sweet," she said. "What a waste."

For the next two days, she lay on the couch holding packs of frozen vegetables against each breast. Sometimes we laughed about it, and she posed for a few sexpot pictures, with the packs of peas pressed against her chest like pasties. Other times, she just stared at the living room wall, adjusting a pack when it slipped. I asked her if her breasts hurt, and she said yes, but not in the way you'd think.

I slid my hand off Dulcie's chest, turned back over, and stared at the T-shirt on the light fixture.

"Did you know," she said, "that when you're at a red light the person next to you probably has a gun in his glove compartment?"

"Defensive driving," I said, trying for a joke.

"Statistically speaking, it's true. Until yesterday, I never thought about how many people have guns," Dulcie said. "Guns in their cars, guns in their pocketbooks when they're going to the market, guns . . . "

A fly was caught between the light and my T-shirt. I could see its shadow darting frantically back and forth until, suddenly, it was gone.

The next evening as I was driving home from work, someone threw an egg at my car. I thought it was another holdup. I sucked in so much air that I started to choke and almost lost control. Two kids then ran by my window. One was wearing a Dracula mask and a cape. The other one had on a rubber monster head and green tights. I'd forgotten it was Halloween.

Dulcie takes holidays pretty seriously, and when I got home I expected to see a cardboard skeleton on the door, and maybe a carved pumpkin or two. Usually she greets the trick-or-treaters wearing a tall black witch hat that she keeps stashed in a closet the rest of the year. When she opens the door, she

makes this funny cackling laugh, which is kind of embarrassing but also sweet. She's so waifish, there's not much about her
that could scare anybody. But when I got home and climbed
the outside stairs to our second-floor apartment, there was
nothing on our door and the apartment was dark.

"What are you doing with all the lights off?" I asked when I
got inside. She was sitting at the kitchen table, her hands
folded in front of her as if she were praying.

"Shut the door," she said. "A whole pack of them just came.
They must have rung the bell five times."

"They want their candy."

"We don't have any."

"Really? You didn't buy any?"

"Charles, we don't know who any of these people are," she
said slowly, as if I were six years old. "I'm not going to open
my door to perfect strangers."

"They're kids."

"What about the ones who come really late?" she asked.
"All those teenagers. They're looking for trouble."

I sat down and reached across the table for her hands. "It's
Halloween, Dulce. It's just kids having fun."

"Plenty of people aren't home on Halloween. This is just
going to be one of those places where nobody's home."

The doorbell rang.

"Dulcie—"

"Sh-h-h!" She hissed at me like a cat.

"This is ridiculous." I got up.

"Please, Charles!"

The bell rang again. I grabbed a box of cookies from the

shelf and went to the door. A little kid was walking away, but he turned back when he heard the door open. He was six, eight years old. An old man I recognized from the neighborhood, maybe his grandfather, stood a few steps behind him.

The boy wore a cowboy outfit—a fringed orange vest over a T-shirt with a picture of Darth Vader on it, jeans mashed down into plastic cowboy boots, and a holster sliding down over his narrow hips. He took a gun out of the holster and waved it around in the air.

"Bang," he said, without enthusiasm.

"You got me," I answered, putting my hands to my chest and pretending to die.

"It's a fake gun," the boy said. "No real bullets."

"You mean I'm not dead?" I tried to sound amazed, and I got a smile out of the kid.

The grandfather said something impatiently in another language, Russian or maybe Armenian.

"Trick or treat," the boy said quietly. He held out a plastic grocery sack with his free hand.

I looked into the bag. There were only a few pieces of candy inside. Suddenly the whole thing made me sad. I offered my box of mint cookies.

The boy looked back at his grandfather, who shook his head. "I'm only allowed to have it if it's wrapped," the boy said to me.

I felt like a criminal. "We didn't have a chance to get to the store," I said, as the boy holstered his gun and moved off with his grandfather.

When I went back inside, Dulcie was standing in the

middle of the dark living room, staring at me. Three months after the baby died, I came home from work and found her standing in that same place. Her belly underneath her T-shirt was huge, much bigger than when she'd actually been pregnant. For one crazy second, I thought that the whole thing had been a mistake, and that she was still pregnant. I felt a kind of relief I had never felt before. Then she lifted her shirt and took out a watermelon from underneath it.

A group of kids yelled "Trick or treat!" below us. They giggled. Someone said "Boo!" then there was a chorus of dutiful thank-you's. I heard small feet pound up the rickety wooden stairway to the second-floor apartments. I walked over to Dulcie and put my arms around her.

"We can't live like this," I said.

"I can," she said.

Dulcie went back to work three days after the carjacking. I dropped her off at school in my car, and she arranged for one of her teacher friends to give her a lift home. I took it as a good sign, her returning to work. She complains about the public school system, all the idiotic bureaucracy she has to deal with, but she loves the kids. She's always coming home with stories about cute things they did, or about how quickly they picked up something she didn't think they'd understand the first time. She was named Teacher of the Year last spring, and a couple of parents got together and gave her this little gold necklace. Her school's in a rough part of Glendale. The necklace was a big deal.

She was home when I got off work, sitting on the couch. She waved a piece of pink paper in the air.

"What's that?" I said.

"We're not allowed to touch the children anymore," she said.

"What are you talking about?"

She told me that a parent had accused a teacher of touching his daughter in the wrong way. Social Services came in, the works. When they finally got around to questioning the girl, she told them the teacher had just patted her on the back because she answered a question right.

"Now the district's in a panic—they don't want a lawsuit every time some kid exaggerates. So, no touching the students."

"That's nuts," I said. "Those kids need to be hugged every once in a while. They probably don't get enough affection at home."

"That's a racist generalization, Charles," she said. "Most of the parents try hard. They love their kids just as much as you and I would."

Neither of us said anything. Dulcie hadn't brought up the idea of our having kids since we'd lost the baby. She had just stepped on a grenade, and I was waiting through those awful seconds before it explodes.

"This is a fucked-up town," she said finally.

I wasn't sure what had made her say this. The school thing? The carjacking?

"Maybe if we turn on the TV we'll catch a freeway chase," I said.

"Or a riot."

"Or a celebrity bio."

She started laughing. "That's the real tragedy," she said. "The celebrity bio."

We laughed some more. When we stopped, neither of us knew what to say.

"I'm not racist," I said at last.

"I know. I didn't mean that."

"I may be prejudiced against celebrities, though."

She squeezed out a smile. It was worth the stupid joke.

The next Saturday, Dulcie called an exterminator. She'd decided that we should pay for one out of our own pocket, because she'd read that some rats carry airborne viruses.

"People died in New Mexico," she said. "Children too."

It turns out that the exterminator you call to get rid of bugs is not the kind you call to get rid of a rat. There's a subspecialty—Rodent Removal. Our rodent remover was named Rod. Rod the Rodent Remover. I was scared of him already.

When he came to the door, he was wearing a clean, pressed uniform with his name on it. "Rod," I said, "thanks for coming."

"It's really Ricardo, but I get more jobs as Rod. Ricardo is too hard for most people to remember. You have a problem with rats?" he said helpfully.

"Yeah. In here." I opened the door wider and led him into the apartment. "It's not really *in* the apartment, but we hear it from in here."

If Ricardo thought it was strange that the mattress was on the living room floor, he didn't say anything. Dulcie was waiting for us in the bedroom.

"It's there," Dulcie said, pointing to a gray smudge where the head of our bed frame met the wall. "He's in there."

Ricardo went over and tapped the wall with his knuckle. Dulcie held her breath. There was no sound from the rat.

"They usually leave the house during the day," Ricardo said.

"How does he get in?" Dulcie said.

Ricardo raised his finger toward the ceiling. "Spanish tile roof. Very pretty, but bad for the rat problem," he said. "They come in through the holes between the tiles."

"So there's nothing we can do?" Dulcie asked, alarmed.

"We can set a trap in the wall through the heating vent there," Ricardo said, pointing to the one vent in our entire apartment, which was, unhelpfully, in the hallway outside our bedroom.

"Then he'll die in the wall?"

"It's a bad smell for a few days, but then it goes away," Ricardo said.

I could see that none of this was making Dulcie feel any better.

"Or I can put a trap on the roof," Ricardo said.

"Do that," Dulcie said quickly.

"Okay," he said. "Now we have a plan."

He reached into his pockets and took out two yellow surgical gloves. Dulcie was horrified, the gloves confirming her suspicions about disease. But Ricardo smiled pleasantly. This was a guy who dealt with rats every day of his life, and it didn't seem to faze him.

"Why do they come inside?" Dulcie said, as we followed

Ricardo towards the door. "The rats. Why do they live in the walls? There's no food there."

"To keep warm," Ricardo said. "Sometimes to have their babies."

He smiled and gave us a courtly nod as I let him out. When I turned back, Dulcie was still staring at the closed door, her hand over her mouth.

"Its' just a rat," I said. I touched her shoulder. She was shaking.

A month after the baby died, the mailman delivered a package that I had to sign for. We don't get a lot of packages, so it was an event. The box was from a company called La Tierra. The name sounded familiar, but I couldn't place it; I was about to call back into the apartment for Dulcie when I remembered. La Tierra was the name of the company that cremated the baby.

"What is it?" Dulcie said from behind me. "Who was at the door?"

I turned around. This will kill her, I thought.

"What is it?" she said again, holding out her hand.

I had no choice but to hand it to her. She looked at it. Her face crumpled. "It's so light," she said finally.

I went to put my arms around her, but she stepped back. Then she started laughing. Her laughter became the kind of giggling you can't turn off. She bit her lips and clenched her teeth, but the giggles kept coming, as if they were tickling her insides in order to get out.

"You probably thought it was something from your mom,"

she said through her laughter. "Or some freebie from a computer company. Oh, my God," she said. "Can you believe this is our life?" I smiled, but it was that weird, embarrassed smile you offer when you feel left out of a joke.

We decided to take the ashes to the beach and scatter them on the water. We drove out to the Ventura County line, to a beach called El Pescador. You have to climb down a steep hillside to get to it, and there's usually no one there, especially in the off season. We parked and scrambled unsteadily down the trail. We were so busy concentrating on not falling that we didn't see the ocean until we were at its level. We both got quiet for a moment. The water was slate gray, pocked by the few white gulls that every so often swooped down to the surface and then rose up again. There were no boats in the ocean, only a couple of prehistoric oil derricks in the distance. "I think we should do it now," Dulcie said.

We opened the box. Inside was some Styrofoam with a hole gouged out. Nestled inside that hole, like a tiny bird, was a plastic bag filled with brown dust. There could not have been more than a tablespoonful. I took the bag and handed the box to Dulcie. Then I kicked off my shoes, rolled up my jeans, and walked out into the water. When I was calf deep, I opened up the bag. I waited for something to happen, for some gust of wind to kick up and take the ashes out to sea. But the day was calm, so I finally dumped the ashes into the water at my feet. A tiny wave moved them towards the shore. I worried that the ashes would end up in the sand, where somebody could step all over them, but then I felt the undertow dragging the water back towards the sea.

"I think that's the bravest thing I've ever seen a person do," Dulcie said as I came out of the water.

As we headed back to the trail, she picked up a smooth stone and slipped it into her pocket. Halfway up the path, she took the stone out and let it drop to the ground.

A week after the holdup, the police called. They had found our stolen car. Once the kids run out of gas, the officer explained, they usually abandon the car rather than pay for more. He gave us the address of the car lot, somewhere in South Central.

"Go early in the morning," the officer warned. "Before they get up."

" 'They'?" I asked.

"You a white guy?" the policeman asked.

"Yeah."

"You want to be down there before wake-up time. Trust me."

Dulcie said it was a self-fulfilling prophecy. Everybody expected things to be bad, so people made them bad. She saw it at her school. The kids who were expected to fail, well, they blew it every time out, even if they knew the work cold.

Still, we took the officer's advice and went down to the lot at seven in the morning. I admit I was nervous, driving through those streets. You like to think you're more open-minded than that, but I guess I'm not. I kept thinking about drive-by shootings and gangs and riots and all the things you read about, thinking, Those things don't happen near where I live, so I'm okay.

We found our car. It was a mess. It had been stripped; even the steering wheel was gone. There was every kind of fast-food wrapper scattered on the back seat, and French fries and old hamburger buns on the floor. You get hungry when you're high. It wasn't worth the price of towing, so we signed it over to the pound and left it there.

As I drove Dulcie to work, I told her the police had asked us to come identify the suspects in a lineup.

"But they'll know it was us who identified them," she said. "They know where we live."

"They were busy getting high. I don't think they were memorizing our address."

"I don't even remember what they looked like. It was dark."

"Once you see some faces, it might come back."

"Charles, don't make me do this. Don't make me!" she cried.

"I'm not going to make you do anything. Jesus. What do you think I am?"

She didn't answer me. I dropped her off at the school. She got out and walked towards the front door, then turned to wave at me, as if it were any regular day, as if we weren't living like some rat trapped in our own wall.

I took the day off. I'd already used up my sick days, and I knew we couldn't throw away the money, but I thought I'd go crazy if I had to be nice to a customer or listen to some technician talk about his bodacious girlfriend or his kid's troubles in school.

I didn't have a plan. I picked up a paper and got breakfast at a hipster coffee shop on Silver Lake Boulevard. There were a lot of tattooed and pierced people eating eggs and bacon; they looked as though they were ending a night, not beginning a day. I tried to concentrate on my paper, but nothing sank in. Then I got back into my car. I ended up driving along Vermont into Griffith Park, past the roads where guys stop to cruise, all the way up to the Observatory. I parked in the empty lot and got out.

The Observatory was closed; it was still early. I was trying to think of something to do with myself when I saw a trail heading up into the hills. The path was well worn; on the weekends, it was usually packed with tourists and families making a cheap day of it. But that morning I had it to myself. I wanted to walk. I walked for hours. I felt the sun rise up, and I saw the darkness that covered the canyons lift, as if someone were sliding a blanket off the ground.

By the time I stopped, others were on the trail—runners, or people walking their dogs, some kids who were probably playing hooky. I looked out over the canyon and thought about how I could go either way: I could stay with Dulcie and be as far away from life as a person could be, or I could leave.

I had been looking forward to the baby. I didn't mind talking to Dulcie about whether or not the kid should sleep in bed with us, or use a pacifier, or how long she would nurse him, or any of the things she could think about happily for days. I got excited about it, too. But I had no idea what it meant. What was real to me was watching Dulcie's body grow bigger and bigger, watching that stripe appear on her belly, watching as her breasts got fuller and that part around her nipples got as wide and dark as pancakes. When the doctors took the baby out of her, they handed him to me without bothering to clean him up; I guess there was no point to it. Every inch of him was perfectly formed. For a second, I thought he would open his eyes and be a baby. It didn't look like anything was wrong with him, like there was any reason for him not to be breathing and crying and getting on with the business of being in the world. I kept saying to myself, This is my baby, this is my baby. But I had no idea what I was saying. The only thing I truly felt was that I would die if something happened to Dulcie.

A runner came towards me on the trail. His face was red, and sweat had made his T-shirt transparent. He gave me a pained smile as he ran past. He kicked a small rock with his shoe, and it flew over the side of the canyon. For some reason, I looked over the edge for the rock. What I saw from where I stood was amazing to me. I saw all kinds of strange cactus plants—tall ones like baseball bats, others like spiky fans. There were dry green eucalyptus trees and a hundred different kinds of bushes I couldn't name. I heard the rustle of animals, skunks or coyotes, maybe even deer. There was garbage on the ground and in the bushes—soda cans, fast-food drink cups, napkins with restaurant logos on them. I saw a condom hanging off a branch, like a burst balloon. For some reason, the garbage didn't bother me. For all I knew, this was one of those mountains that was made of trash, and it was nature that didn't belong. Maybe the trash, the dirt, the plants, bugs, condoms—maybe they were all just fighting for a little space.

I got home before Dulcie. I dragged the mattress back into the bedroom. I took my shirt off the light fixture in the living room and put it in the dresser. When Dulcie came back, she

saw what I had done, but she didn't say anything. We ate dinner early. I watched a soccer game while she corrected papers.
Then I turned off the lights in the living room, and we went
into the bedroom. She knew my mind was made up, and she
climbed into bed like a soldier following orders. When I
snapped off the bedside lamp, she gave a little gasp.

We lay quietly for a while, getting used to the dark. We listened for the rat, but he wasn't there.

"You think the traps worked?" she said.

"Maybe."

I reached for her. At first it was awkward, as though we were
two people who had never had sex with each other. Truthfully,
I was half ready for her to push me away. But she didn't, and,
after a while, things became familiar again. When I rolled on
top of her, though, I felt her tense up underneath me. She
started to speak. "I should go and get—"

I put my fingers on her mouth to stop her. "It's okay," I said.

She looked up at me with her big watery eyes. She was ter-
rified. She started again to say something about her diaphragm.
I stopped her once more.

"It's okay," I repeated.

I could feel her heart beating on my skin. I could feel my
own heart beating even harder. We were scared, but we kept
going.

THIEF

A bird has flown into my house and nested in the middle of the living room. The whorls of dried leaves and sticks look close and protective as cupped hands. I consider whether a bird in the house is good luck or bad. As a younger woman I was practical and would walk carelessly under ladders and on top of cracks. But seventeen years ago, when my beautiful son was born with a hole in his heart and undeveloped muscles in his legs, I began to believe in casual magic. A light going out of its own in the middle of a decisive marital argument or the sight of the spring's first jacaranda spreading its purple umbrella on the day of an operation became reassuring signs that the world provides its own sort of order. Believing this does me just as much good as knowing that x percent of children born with a hole in the heart might not make it to their thirties; information that turns out to be impractical as any kind of guideline. A bird in the house, it occurs to me, might offer direction for this next stretch of life I'm staring down at like a novice skier at the top of a sheer trail: Billy, my only child, wheelchair-bound and weak of heart, is going north to college in two days. But I can't remember about the bird's significance and the tufted nest begins to look sepulchral. Well, if it is a bad sign, no matter, because I have become a friend to bad luck. I know it intimately enough to feel comforted by its presence.

Through the open door that leads into the attached garage, I can hear Billy grunting his way from the passenger seat to his wheelchair. I imagine his newly mannish arm muscles straining under the dead weight of his useless legs. I left him alone in the garage with the excuse of wanting to get his new suitcase into his room right away so he could begin packing. In truth, I couldn't watch him struggle one minute longer without moving in to take charge of his body as I have done all his life. Ever since his scholarship came through, Billy has become adamant that I not be his shortcut anymore. I am not allowed to push him around tight curves, get the milk down from the refrigerator, even retrieve a book he's left in the living room when he's already made the acrobatic transition to bed.

I stare another minute at the nest, only now taking in the waffle-patterned footprints that lead from it down the hall towards the bedrooms. It occurs to me that I am the only one in the house capable of leaving footprints and that I have no shoes with waffle soles. And then, as though knowledge informs the muscles first, I move dumbly in the direction of those prints.

I stand in my open bedroom door, trying to comprehend the tangle of flung clothing and sheets. The dresser drawers hang open like mouths. My jewelry box lies empty on the floor, ten feet away from the night table where it normally rests. One pillow has been stripped of its case and sits at the foot of the bed. Its soft yellowing mass is folded over on itself as though it has been punched in the gut. Moments later, when I'm standing in my kitchen staring at the torn-out center of the plate-glass window, I realize we have been robbed. Shards of safety glass hang from the ragged hole like sticky candy.

Billy wheels up, takes in the window, then rolls to the low-hanging phone and dials 911. He's impatient and efficient. He will not suffer sports-analogy-making doctors ("the operation was a double, we're looking for a home run") and falsely optimistic therapists. His precision of thought is an antidote to the wild ambiguity of his body. For instance, now: Billy registers the fact of the robbery and moves to the next logical step of calling the police, while I am still wondering whether, had I stayed in the garage with him, this whole thing might never have happened.

"Busy," Billy says incredulously. He pushes down the disconnect button with his finger, then lifts it to try again. He makes another thwarted attempt while I study the hole, trying to imagine how a body could fit through the tiny aperture; it is like the paradox of birth. And then I gasp at the realization that this agile thief might still be in the house.

"Billy," I whisper, "we have to get out of here!"

He waves off my anxiety, as though the very caution that has kept him thriving all these years is now something he thinks might actually harm him.

"He could still be in the house," I say, more forcefully.

Billy hangs up the phone fully this time, shaking his head. He has dark, glittering eyes and a cunning smile that appears when people lie in his presence. *It's good to see you*, they'll say brightly, when, in truth, they can't wait to get away from this reminder of life's mistakes.

"Good old 911," he says, tucking an auburn lock behind his ear. "Always there when you need them."

I remember an episode ten years earlier when it had taken so long for the paramedics to reach our hillside house that they found me holding an exposed electrical wire over Billy's bare chest, ready to shock his ragged heart back into a normal rhythm myself. "Let's go," I say. "We'll call 911 from across the street."

"Mom," Billy says, irritation breaking the word into three syllables.

"Billy, now!" I command and am gratified to see him hunch his broad shoulders in childlike acquiescence and obey.

I open the front door and walk down the steps of the porch. Richard, my ex-husband, built the wooden stairs himself twenty years ago in an effort to add grace to the pitiable warren of rooms we were able to afford. I had grand ideas of doing something countryish with the house. I ripped out pictures from home magazines and spent weekends painting the exterior barn-red. The rest of the plans were stalled by lack of funds, pregnancy, and then Billy. Now Billy rolls down the ramp Richard added when we got the first tiny wheelchair and pragmatism became our ruling aesthetic.

Billy rushes ahead of me as I reach into my purse for the keys to the courtyard door. The eight-foot stucco wall surrounding the house has been useless today. Billy maneuvers his chair with the quick, restless movements that have become his signature lately. The summer has been hot and tedious, made all the more grueling by his impatience to leave for college and my growing distress about this same event. I have tried to coach him in the possible scenarios awaiting him: if he feels faint, he must call the doctor I've lined up in San Francisco; if his leg muscles seize up, he must administer his own massage. I've plied him with lists of clinics and on-campus organizations and friends in the area who he can call in an emergency. He has listened to me restlessly and I've had to refrain from forcing him to look me in the eye and repeat what I've said.

A sharp movement behind the lemon tree catches my eye and makes me stop. I see the flash of skin and an unnatural cobalt blue that can only be clothing.

"Are we going or staying?" Billy asks from the garden door.

I consider saying nothing and simply continuing to the door and leaving. But the idea of letting this thief stay in my garden while my son and I run away like frightened mice enrages me.

"You there!" I call out.

"Mom?" Billy asks, and I hear the whir of him backing up, pivoting, then motoring towards me.

"Come out from there," I demand.

I step in front of Billy to protect him just as the figure appears out of the bushes.

It is a girl. She crouches, avoiding the low-hanging branches and their cumbersome lemons. Her brown hair, streaked with magenta dye, parts to reveal a pale swath of forehead and a round, harshly made-up face. Her fists are clenched in front of her chest. She glares at me, as if I have interrupted her.

She wears a blue ribbed tank top, and the straps of a faded tiger-print bra poke out from the arm holes. The bra itself is tight, forcing the skin underneath the shirt to pucker. Little pillows of flesh bulge at the crease of her underarms. An ornate dragon tattoo writhes up one arm. Its open, fiery mouth lands squarely on the girl's shoulder as if ready to take a bite out of her neck. Her mouth is full and down-turned, traced with a dark maroon lip pencil that shows more distinctly where her lipstick has worn off. She is on the outer edge of girlhood, maybe even Billy's age, but her adolescence lingers around her like smoke.

"Don't hurt me," she says. Her voice is raw and full of grit.

A volcano of adrenaline erupts from my gut. "You bitch!" I scream. "What the hell do you think you're doing in my house? What did you take?"

"Nothing," she says flatly.

"Give it back. Now!"

"I said I didn't get anything."

"My jewelry box is empty. My drawers are wide open!"

"My friend took the stuff."

The mention of an accomplice makes me scared and I step back, nearly knocking into Billy's knees. I'm overcome by my stupidity. I might as well have wheeled my son into the middle of freeway traffic. After all these years of vigilance, my irresponsibility weakens me.

"Where is this friend?" I ask hoarsely

"Gone."

"How? The garden door is locked."

"The same way we got in," she says, gesturing back towards the wall where dirt adheres to the rough stucco, footprints of the nimble climber. The girl takes a step forwards, then cries out in pain. She steadies herself on the branch of the tree.

"What's wrong with you?" Billy asks.

"I twisted my ankle trying to get over your wall. What's wrong with you?"

The question startles both Billy and me. We are used to people traveling wide arcs around Billy's disability, or feigning disinterest, as though his condition were something only vaguely notable, like a breeze.

"I'm a cripple," Billy says finally. "I can't walk."

"Ever?" she asks.

"Not so far," he answers dryly. "But we can always pray for a miracle."

The girl does not respond at first, but then a small, angry smile darts briefly across her face. "Take it from me," she says. "Don't waste your time."

Billy does not take his eyes from her.

"Get the hell out of my yard," I snarl.

She takes another step and falters on the uneven dirt, wincing and cursing.

"She's hurt," Billy says.

"I said get out!"

Tears burst from her eyes as she puts pressure on the bad leg and begins to limp towards the garden door. Midway across the patio, she collapses to the ground, then half crawls, half drags herself the rest of the way.

"Jesus, Mother. Help her!"

At the door, the girl grabs onto the metal latch and pulls herself up, then tries to open the door. It is locked; I have the key.

"What do you want me to do here?" she demands, turning back to me. Then all the color drains from her face. She drops to the ground and passes out.

Despite my resistance, Billy insists that we take the girl into the house. We manage this by laying her head and torso across Billy's lap. I hold her legs while Billy wheels her up the ramp. She nearly falls off her perch more than once, and Billy has to grasp her thigh and buttock with one hand while maneuvering the chair with the other. The effort exhausts him, but he is determined. He jiggers the chair back and forth in order to attack the ramp from the right angle. The muscles in his jaw work as he makes the minute calculations that are necessary.

When we have gotten the girl into the living room, we roll her awkwardly onto the couch. Billy wraps ice in a towel, then lays it on her swelling ankle. Afterwards, he collects some throw pillows and props them under her head. He lifts her shoulders gently, careful not to snag her hair.

"What are we going to do with her now?" I ask.

"Take care of her." His reply is a challenge.

"And then what?"

He has no answer, which makes me feel haughtily victorious and then sad. Billy and I, once a team, now hunker in opposing camps, defending ourselves against the rupture we know is coming. We pick fights, become annoyed by one another's long-standing habits, knowing no more graceful way to call it quits.

"We should phone the police," I tell him. I silently add this next call to all the ones I have made before it, to doctors and home nurses, cleaning women and tutors, and, at one time, a husband. These people have all come and eventually left, satisfied that the momentary problems for which they'd been required were neatly solved. What they left behind, besides newly hung packets of I.V. fluid, folded towels, and homework, was loneliness. Taking care of Billy has been solitary work. I start for the phone.

"Don't do it, Mother."

I am about to fight back, but I stop myself. Billy's assertiveness is new. If he could, he would bound out of that chair and wrestle me to the ground. To ignore him now would be to cruelly take advantage of him.

After ten minutes, the girl's eyes flutter open. She lifts her head off the pillows, takes in her situation, then lets it fall back heavily. "You called the cops," she says, exhaling. "Fuck me."

"We didn't call the cops," Billy says.

"Why not? What do you people want from me?"

"What I want," I say, eyeing the girl's tattoo, "is for you to tell me why you did this to us."

Of course it was drugs, although the girl claims they were not for her but for her boyfriend. Cocaine makes her nervous, she says.

"So, you're willing to commit robbery for your boyfriend's bad habit?" I ask.

"You don't know anything about him."

"He left you stranded."

"Shut up."

"He took my jewelry."

"Sorry," she says, not meaning it.

"You could get the jewelry back for her," Billy says to the girl.

"I doubt it. It's probably already on the street."

"So fast?" I say, shocked. "It can't have been more than an hour."

"He's looking to score some drugs, not make an offer on a house."

I suck in an audible breath of air as I imagine my jewelry being pawed over by gangsters in flashy clothes and heavy-framed sunglasses, my life turning into a dated police drama.

"What's your name?" Billy asks.

The girl looks suspicious.

"Jesus, don't you get it?" he says, exasperated. "You're getting off. We're not turning you in."

"My name is Babe," she answers. She sits up and moves her legs with difficulty. "I'm fucked up big time," she mumbles, lifting the towel of ice and staring at her red and purple ankle. "Oh, my God!" she exclaims at the angry bulge.

I'm startled too. Her foot looks terrible. "You should see a doctor," I tell her, moving closer to inspect the foot. "Why don't you call someone to come and take you to an emergency room?"

"My chauffeur, you mean?"

"How about parents?" I offer, ignoring her sarcasm.

"Parent," she corrects. "And she wouldn't exactly . . . cope with this situation, if you know what I mean."

"The situation of finding out her kid is a thief?"

Babe judges me narrowly, as if she's wondering whether she might be better off with the cops. "In an emergency," she says finally. "She's not good in an emergency, okay? Christ, what is this, Court TV?"

This elicits a yelp of laughter from Billy.

"Listen," I interrupt. "We've helped you out. You need to go now."

"Call your boyfriend," Billy adds. He looks at her steadily, waiting to see how she'll meet this challenge.

"Phone?" she responds, holding out an expectant hand while she stares him down.

Billy spins his chair dexterously and heads for the portable phone across the room. Returning, he hands it to Babe, his eyes dancing with delight.

She presses the buttons. While she waits, she reaches up under her tank top and adjusts her bra. "Poppy, you fuck," she says finally into the phone. "You fucking left me here. . . . I broke my fucking foot or something. . . . " She begins to cry. Tears flood her eyes and mucus clogs her nose. Her voice rises up until it is a high squeal. Billy turns away. He wheels himself to the other side of the room and pretends to investigate the CDs.

"You have to come and get me, Poppy," Babe wails. "You have to. If I don't get out of here, I'll——," She holds the phone out and stares at it angrily. "The machine cut me off," she says in disbelief. She throws the phone down on the couch and covers her face with her hands and lets out a muted roar.

"We'll take you to the hospital," I offer.

"Please," she says, lowering her hands from her face. Her skin is blotchy and little dark tributaries of eye makeup run down her cheeks. "Just let me lie here a little while longer. I'll be okay if I can just lie here." She lays back, shuts her eyes, and sinks quickly into an exhausted sleep.

"Maybe we should tell Dad," Billy says.

This takes me by surprise. Richard has been dutiful about taking Billy alternate weekends and Wednesday nights, but it has been years since he has been involved in any of the day-to-day decisions of our lives. He would say this began even before we split. My relentless efficiency seemed to denature him: the more I took charge, hunting down specialists, reading up on therapies, the more Richard retreated. It frightened him to acknowledge there could be more and better to do for our son, an admission that we had not done enough already. Our relationship, at one time merely shadowed by Billy's needs, became eclipsed by them until we were no more to one another than co-workers, barking orders and complaining when the other did not do his share. When he had an affair, we spoke obligatorily about resurrecting our marriage, but by then we had moved too far from one another to find any obvious way back. I've had short-lived relationships since, enough to satisfy occasional longing, but nothing that has come close to permanence.

"I don't think your father can do anything in this situation," I answer finally.

"I'm going to go pack," Billy says.

"Do you need me?"

"No." He turns and disappears down the hallway. I listen for the customary *thwock* as his chair hits his bedroom door's threshold. When it comes, I think only of its absence.

An imperfect baby is like a grenade. In the moment when Billy emerged with bluish skin and legs flaccid as rope, everyone in the delivery room held his astonished breath as though, together, we could stop time, push that baby back inside, and pull out the right one instead. And then the room erupted into a melee of activity as strangers rushed in and out with frantic precision and my baby was rolled away on a trolley like an unwanted dessert.

Richard ran after Billy and I was left alone with the doctor, who delivered the afterbirth, not daring to lift his eyes. I did not know him; I delivered at a clinic and this exhausted young man happened to be the doctor on duty. But suddenly I found myself studying the wide part in his hair, trying to find something familiar there. When he finished sewing, he took off his medical gloves and spoke to me. I watched his lips move but could not hear his words, could not hear my own voice as I said, "Thank you, Doctor," hoping that gratitude might improve my baby's situation. When he left, a nurse came to clean me up. She straightened a sheet over my exposed crotch. She said things too, but my head was filled with a sucking noise, like a vacuum. When she left, no one came back into the room for nearly half an hour. I lay on the delivery table, scratching my skin like a drug addict as the epidural wore off.

Billy survived the birth and the many operations and therapies that left him with a heart that worked well enough ("A used Nissan, not a Caddy," one doctor had said) and legs that would not work at all. Better than the opposite, I reminded myself in those early years when comparative bad luck became the calculus of my life. I'd walk Billy in the mall, braving the sorry looks of shoppers and the uncomfortable salespeople. And just as I would be about to make for the nearest wheel-chair exit, my bravery spent, I would see another affected child and think: It could be worse. The truth is, Billy is fine. Although he has had moments of frustration and self-pity, he accepts his wheelchair as I do my legs; it is simply the thing that gets him from here to there. He is as wondrous and ener-vating as any son and I've learned to overlook his disabilities in order to scold when he needs scolding, and praise him for his accomplishments without qualification. He may live longer than everybody or he may die young; there is no way of pre-dicting and I have trained myself to envision his life, not his death. But still, I think about his heart all the time, that slip-pery pink bladder. I think about it driving in the car as a radio song throbs to the rhythm of his pulse. I think about it during the hours I work as a part-time paralegal, my pencil tapping with bored impatience to Billy's beat. I am like a worried air-plane passenger who valiantly stays awake to support the unaware pilot: if I cease to imagine Billy's heart, it might stop altogether.

Babe sits up out of her sleep as if instructed by her dreams. She stares wild-eyed through matted hair. Her shirt has become twisted around her waist, exposing her entire belly, including the bottom portion of her bra. Billy wheels himself into the room a second later, his eyes instantly magnetized towards that pale, soft flesh. She sees his gaze but makes no move to cover herself.

"I passed out."

"For, like, an hour," Billy says. I cringe at his uncharacteristic Valley speak.

"Wow," Babe says, looking around. "I'm still here."

"I'm cooking dinner," I announce, "and then we'll see about getting you to a doctor."

"So it turns out you're not a witch, after all," she says.

I take a deep breath and head for the kitchen. "There's a hole in my window," I call back over my shoulder and am satisfied by the embarrassed silence that answers back.

Ten minutes later, I hear laughter from the living room. I come out to find Billy, sitting on the couch, his legs splayed as limply as a marionette's while Babe spins around the room in his wheelchair. She laughs, fiddling with the motor control as though it is the joystick of a video game. The frenzy is narcotic: whizzing around the room, she barely misses the coffee table and does not miss a wooden chair, which topples over. She covers her mouth with her hands but her eyes betray her delight. Billy smiles broadly, calling out instructions like a frantic father giving a driving lesson. He laughs as she careens into a wall.

"You might," I yell over the noise, "think about cleaning up my room."

They stop and look at me as though my identity stumps them. Finally, Babe rolls over to the couch. She heads straight for Billy's legs, stopping the chair short just as her knees make contact with his. She places her hands on his thighs, using them for support as she pushes herself out of the chair.

"Feel anything?" she asks huskily, her hands sliding a few inches higher.

"I'm not numb, if that's what you mean."

"That's exactly what I mean," she says, her hands nearly touching his crotch. Billy doesn't flinch. Then she pivots her body out of the chair and onto the couch next to him, all the while managing to avoid putting pressure on her foot. She waits patiently while Billy hoists himself into his chair. Getting himself up from the cushions is awkward and I have to stop myself from reaching out to help. When he finally manages the task, he slings his legs onto their rests with showy confidence. He could be backing up a car, his hand behind a girl's hot neck, or reaching up to pick a football out of the air without breaking stride as he jogs past an admiring date. Babe, using the back of the wheelchair as a crutch, follows him down the hall towards my room.

She's voluble at dinner. She tells us that she's lived all over the country, only coming to Los Angeles a year ago when she was sixteen. She explains that her house burned down and that she and her mother lived in a shelter for five months. Her story is improbable and I try to mask my disbelief.

"Now we live at the Sea Spray on Ventura. It's a motel. You probably passed it a million times."

"What sea exactly sprays on Ventura Boulevard?" Billy asks cannily.

"Hey, there's a pool," Babe says defensively. "My mother cleans the place, so we get a room for free." She takes a giant bite out of her hamburger.

Billy is riveted. Other people's lives are like travel to him. This one is like a trip to some exotic land.

"That's quite a story," I say.

She laughs and ketchup trickles down her chin. She licks it off with her tongue. "Everyone always wants your life to be a movie, like it only counts if it has enough good parts to keep them interested. You know what I'd give for a boring life like you have?"

"What would you give?" I ask.

"It's just an expression," she says witheringly.

"If you want a boring life," Billy says, "you could start by not dating drug addicts and breaking into other people's houses."

"Yeah," she agrees. "Poppy's something else. He makes me lose my mind."

Billy is silent. He's never had a girlfriend that I know of. Girls call the house for help with homework. He and his friends go to the movies in packs like nervous dogs.

"Where's the dad in this picture?" Babe asks.

"I think that's not your business," I say.

"I get it. I have to tell you all my secrets because I'm the hostage. But you don't have to tell me anything."

"You're not a hostage," I say.

"He left," Billy interrupts. "He's remarried."

"Umm," she muses, regarding me as if she knows my entire story. "My mother has bad taste in men too. It's unbelievable."

"Runs in the family," Billy says.

"Poppy's all right. He's trying to get off the stuff. People fuck up all the time. It's the history of the world."

"You're pretty smart," Billy says. "You should go to college."

She breaks out into a wide grin. "Give me some money!"

"We don't have any money," he says.

"Bullshit," she says, laughing. "Look at this place."

She waves her hand around the room and I follow it, taking in our yard-sale furniture, our sun-bleached rug, the knick-knacks that I've been too tired to throw out over the years.

"You broke into the wrong house," I tell her. "Next time, try Beverly Hills."

"Damn," she says, smiling ruefully. "I thought this *was* Beverly Hills."

I laugh, despite myself.

"Just like I told you," she says. "The history of the world."

After dinner, I stay in the kitchen, washing the dishes, while Babe and Billy talk in the living room. I hear some music start up, an old Linda Ronstadt tape of mine that Billy considers "girl music." I spend fifteen more minutes cleaning up the broken glass on the floor and carefully picking the loose shards from the hole. I try to repair the window temporarily with a piece of cardboard torn from the back of a legal pad, but the cardboard is much too small to do the job and I give up. Thinking of the cost of a new window makes me angry. I head for the living room, determined to carry Babe out of the house if I have to. But the room is empty and, aside from the music, the house is oddly quiet. I listen for the sound of Billy's chair or Babe's low, scratchy voice, but hear nothing.

I walk down the hallway until I am standing before Billy's half-closed door. I cannot help but put my face up to the crack. Billy is sitting in his chair while Babe, kneeling in front of him, works her face into his lap. His hands are on her head, guiding her. I start to back away but my hand brushes against the door, opening it farther. Billy turns in my direction. At first I cannot tell if he sees me but when he lifts his hands from Babe's head and covers his own face, I know he has.

I retreat into the kitchen and stand next to the broken window. I try to steady my shaking body by breathing night air deep into my lungs. As I exhale, I imagine the ribbon of air leaving me through this jagged hole as if it is being dragged away, like a baby on a pint-sized gurney. It occurs to me that a child is something that gets stolen bit by bit. A two-year-old dissolves into a five-year-old, and no picture can adequately bring back the feel of him, the sound of his voice, and all the intangible qualities that made him himself at that moment. A ten-year-old becomes fifteen, then seventeen. Then he slips out of your life altogether and the baby who once required your endless gaze now covers his eyes.

No one speaks as the three of us drive down the hill. Billy sits in the passenger seat, staring out the windshield into the dark night. Babe slumps behind me, stretching her injured leg over the back seat.

"Listen," she says, as we emerge into the brightness of Ventura Boulevard. "Forget the emergency room. Maybe you should just take me home."

"Your foot could be broken," I say. "You should have it x-rayed."

"I don't need an X ray."

"Whatever you want," I answer.

"That's what I want."

She directs me down the boulevard a few miles until we reach a motel. From the outside, it looks bleak: a fifties-style affair barely resuscitated. "Sea Spray" flashes in neon, boom-erang-shaped letters. When we turn into the court, things look a bit more hopeful. Someone has taken the time to plant some palms in the concrete planter in the center of the driveway. And there's that pool glimmering in the safety lights.

As soon as Babe gets out, I put the car into gear. She jumps, startled, as if she didn't expect to be abandoned. She leans into the car window, looking across me towards Billy. "See you around."

"People say that all the time," he says quietly, looking down, "but it's usually not true." He lifts his head now and meets her gaze with a shrug. Babe's eyes shine wetly like the pool, but before I can tell what she's feeling, her face hardens and she draws back into herself. She straightens up and tosses her hair behind her back with a flick of her head.

"See you never," she says and turns away from the car.

I drive around the circular driveway. We pass her one more time as she hobbles across the pavement before we head back onto the boulevard.

I do see Babe once more, three months later, when I stop at a grocery store in North Hollywood I don't usually shop at. I'm picking up some decent coffee before I head to the law office where I've started a new full-time job. I don't notice her until I am at the head of my checkout line, ready to pay. She's the cashier.

"Holy shit," she says, looking around nervously.

She drags my bag of coffee slowly over the scanner, then holds on to it for an extra moment, as though she's forgotten what comes next. Neither of us speaks. The woman in back of me starts to pile her food onto the conveyer belt. I hand Babe some money. She searches my face, looking for some clue as to how to proceed, but my expression must mirror her own uncertainty. Pressing some buttons on her register, she makes the change.

"Paper or plastic?" she asks, holding up the coffee.

"Plastic."

She reaches for a bag and shakes it open. "How's your son?"

"He's up at school now."

"I thought about his heart one time. I pictured it kind of dented, like the cans of tuna fish they stick at the back of the shelf."

"It's not dented."

"Oh," she says, looking down, ashamed of her ignorance.

"Can I have my coffee?"

When she hands me the bag, I notice the tail of her dragon tattoo peeking out from beneath her long-sleeved uniform blouse. At her wrist is my silver bracelet inlaid with polished green stones. I start to say something when it occurs to me that the bracelet isn't mine to take back anymore. Saying good-bye, I leave the store.

I sit in my parked car for a few minutes without starting it, watching the suburban ballet out my window. A mother straps her baby into a car seat, an old man shuffles his patient way towards the sliding doors. He passes a woman in a half cape and a nurse's outfit who's trying to collect money for the homeless.

I talk to Billy once a week. He tells me just enough information to quiet me. He sounds happy and busy; there's often raucous laughter in the background of our calls. In the beginning I worried about his health, wondering each morning if he'd taken his medication and done his exercises. But lately, whole days go by when I don't think about him at all.

FALLING BODIES

Will sat in his basement, mending his shortwave radio, when two floors above, his grandson cried out. The sound, a high and sharp bark followed by an attenuated wail, reached Will like a distant siren—he took notice of it, but it was someone else's emergency. Still, unable to concentrate, he put down his pliers and waited for Beth to quiet Ethan's cries. He told himself there was nothing he could do to help; he had no talent for comfort. He reminded himself too that the baby might not even be his grandchild at all. There was no proof, only Beth's word, and he found this, as with everything else about the girl, untrustworthy. His own son, Michael, had died a full year earlier without knowing about the pregnancy, so there was no one to corroborate Beth's claim. For all Will knew, the fact of his grandfatherhood could simply be the fabrication of a girl in desperate straits.

He had met Beth only once before she had come to live with him, at the funeral in Yosemite. The service took place in view of the peak from which Michael, a professional rescue climber, had fallen. Will was struck by how young Beth looked—she seemed barely out of her teens. Her body was dwarfed by a heavy woolen poncho and she repeatedly blew an unruly strand of hair away from her forehead, as if exasperated by the eulogies.

She'd introduced herself briefly after the ceremony. "I'm Michael's almost-ex-girlfriend," she'd said. "We were going to break up, but we didn't get around to it."

Will nodded, not wanting to expose his ignorance about Michael's life. Then, in order to avoid further conversation, he handed her his business card. He never imagined that, a year later, he would receive a phone call as a result.

"I thought I could make it alone," she'd said bluntly, her voice sounding even more pinched and girlish over the phone than in person. "But with a baby, no way. You're his grandfather, so help me out." Her utter assurance had made him agree immediately to her demand.

Now the child's cries subsided and the house fell quiet once again. Will tried to focus on his radio. A few minutes later, however, Beth appeared in the basement doorway, her unkempt hair partly obscuring her small, grave face. She clutched the now-alert Ethan against one hip, while a colorful bouquet of laundry threatened to burst from her other arm.

"Nightmare," she said, tilting her head towards the baby. "How can a four-month-old have bad dreams?"

Will stood immediately, a courtesy he regretted. Ever since Beth had come, he had not felt relaxed in his own home. When she entered a room, he felt caught, as if he had been drinking milk from the carton or reading pornography. She judged him wordlessly, with a bemused and pitying smile. He could not even empty the coffee grounds from the filter without thinking how ridiculous he must look to her, bent over a scuffed plastic garbage pail, his slacks easing down his backside.

Lit by the spill coming from the doorway, Beth's legs and the line of her underwear were visible through her nightgown. Her lack of restraint unnerved Will. She reminded him of a cat, casually licking its genitals in a puddle of midday sun. She was uninhibited, making her way to the bathroom with blemished face and musty breath, or picking a piece of food from between her gapped front teeth at the dinner table. She didn't seem to care what he thought of her; in fact, she didn't seem to care about him at all. The laundry was a perfect example: without asking his permission, she had made use of the bathroom hamper, but sorted out her and the baby's clothes when it was time to do a load, as if Will's did not require washing as well. He had to suppress his discomfort at the idea of her touching his dirty shirts and underwear.

"Be careful," Will said, moving towards the stairs. "There's a tread I keep meaning to fix." He motioned to a board that had popped loose from its nails months earlier. He had considered jerry-rigging a quick replacement, but knew that the whole staircase was warped and needed to be rebuilt. It was a big job and he had decided to wait until the January rains came, when work would slow at his equipment rental shop.

He reached out to take the laundry from Beth.

"I got it," she said, shaking him off. She could barely see over her load, but stepped carefully past the weak tread as though she had an animal alertness that kept her from danger. Reaching the landing, she let the laundry fall in a pile at her feet, then shifted Ethan to her other hip. Beth crouched down and began to sort the darks from the lights with her free hand while Ethan bobbled back and forth at her side. When she was finished, she stood, eyeing Will's radio suspiciously.

"I know what that thing is," she announced. "It's a CB, like people have in their trucks so they can speed and get away with it."

"Not really. This is a more complicated piece of equipment. Sometimes I can tune in to another country altogether."

"Why would you want to do a thing like that?"

He thought of a handful of reasons he could give her, everything from the complicated mechanics involved in building a shortwave from parts, to his long-standing interest in radio communication. He used to share this sort of information with his wife, who took his interest seriously. But she had been dead three years now.

The baby turned and studied Will, who could not help interpreting the wariness of the child's gaze, as if Ethan knew that he and Will were not blood relations.

"I don't have a thing for machines," Beth said finally. "They bore me to death."

"I guess you could say I'm a gadget man."

"Gadg-it," she said. The word fell apart in the air, becoming nothing more than a random collision of sounds. Will felt her utter dismissal of him. She reached down for her laundry, tossing the darks into the machine.

"Put the powder in first. You get a better distribution of soap that way," he said. He realized how ridiculous he must sound to a careless girl like Beth. But he could not watch a job being done improperly without trying to make corrections. This was a tic of his, something his wife had learned to abide generously, one that had driven his son, five years earlier, out of his house for good. "The machine works best that way," he added.

"Really?" she said indifferently.

"It's designed so that water comes up from the bottom to dissolve the soap," Will continued. "It's efficient."

He took great pleasure in understanding the way things worked. He had owned his rental shop for thirty years, leasing out the heavy tools and machines people needed when they wanted to fix their homes or yards themselves. Before buying a piece of equipment, he carefully studied the specs, trying to figure out how the device was made, and how he might improve it if it were his to invent all over again. He believed that a tool built using simple logic was the most effective. When a machine broke down, he knew there was no quick fix; there was something convoluted about the way it was put together in the first place.

Beth shook the powder on top of the clothes and a plume of dust rose out of the machine, causing Ethan to cough. She pulled his face towards her chest. "Oh, well," she said, fanning the air. "I guess I blew it again."

The laundry machine belched into its wash cycle. She carried Ethan to Will's worktable and began circling the radio as though it were prey. Will stepped back to make room for her when she passed. They had touched only a few times, a brief awkward hug when she had first arrived in L.A., the occasional press of skin on the rare occasions when she handed him the baby. Her nearness made him tense.

"What's the farthest-away place you've ever heard?" she asked.

"I got Australia once."

"Big deal. They speak English in Australia."

"I got some French a few months back."

"Could've been Canada."

"It wasn't. It was France."

"Could have been Louisiana," she said. "They speak French there too. Michael was going to take me to New Orleans, but he didn't."

In the month since her arrival, she had made casual references to Michael, once mentioning a particular song he had liked, another time complaining that he loved mountains more than women. To have Michael known more intimately by this stranger only emphasized how little Will knew his son. He would mull over these teases of information for days, as though he could clone a whole person out of a few predilections.

There had been no climactic moment of rupture between Will and his son, only a slowly accumulating density of criticism and recrimination. Michael, a respectful and dutiful child, became a confounding youth. He spent his nights under the spell of horsepower, his days as a secret agent, dragging phones into bathrooms and speaking in an incomprehensible teenage code. If Will tried to talk to his son about school, Michael would answer in monosyllables. When the topic of his future was raised, Michael's listless, heavy-lidded eyes would shame Will out of continuing. Still, Will could not help but pry and poke at his son, as he tried to kick the mechanism that had once functioned so beautifully back into gear. The result was Michael's decision to forgo college and move up north right after graduation. Even then, Will had argued that Michael was too tall to be a climber. Michael had not put up an argument, but simply cast a resigned look towards his mother and left the room. Will realized, then, that his son had departed years earlier. Will had simply failed to notice.

"Turn the radio on," Beth commanded. "Let's see if it works."

"We'll wake the baby," Will said, gesturing to the child, who had fallen asleep, his whole body crumpled in Beth's arm like a deflated balloon.

"Oh, c'mon," she whined. "I'm so bored here. Give me something to hold my interest."

Reluctantly, Will hooked up his radio. Under her gaze, his normally deft touch escaped him. He could not hone in on anything but static. Finally, a thin voice pierced through the fuzz.

"That guy?" a woman said. "I wouldn't let him get one over on me, I'll tell you that much. I'm no E ticket at Disneyland, okay?"

"Whooee!" Beth cried out. "Oops," she whispered guiltily

as the baby stirred. When he settled back into sleep, she turned her attention again to the radio.

"I'm no slut," the woman continued. "I want to be wined and dined, the whole routine, before I give it up."

"Where do you think she is?" Beth said with hushed fascination. "She could be anywhere, right? Idaho, or England?"

"She's right here in North Hollywood. It's a local phone line. I've heard it before." Will switched off the radio.

Beth seemed momentarily disappointed, but then brightened. "So, you listen to her phone calls?" she asked, her eyes registering the delight she took in his transgression.

"I pass the signal, now and then," he said.

This was not the truth. He knew quite a lot about the woman on the radio, and had listened in on her more frequently than he knew was proper. Her name was Louise and her conversations had mainly to do with men. She'd either be talking to one in a flirtatious tone of voice or talking disdainfully about one to a girlfriend. What held Will's interest, beyond the blatantly sexual nature of the calls, was the fact that Louise was a liar. In one conversation she might throw herself at a man in a way that both excited and embarrassed Will. Then she would turn around and tell a friend how she couldn't wait for this pathetic sap to stop pestering her.

"Isn't it illegal?" Beth said. "Listening in like this?"

"Of course not."

"I think it's illegal. It's like spying. You're like a Peeping Tom. God!" she exclaimed with relish.

"I'm not a Peeping Tom," he said, trying to mask his dislike for Beth. "The world's not such a private place as you think it is. Somebody can find out everything they need to know about you just by having your credit card."

"I don't have a credit card!" she announced triumphantly, as though she had beaten the system through craft rather than fiscal irresponsibility.

The baby woke up, his tetchy cry turning into a full-scale scream.

"I better feed him before my tits explode, anyway," Beth sighed, fingering the top button of her nightgown. When she noticed Will's alarm, she grinned. "Don't worry, I won't flash you," she said, then climbed the stairs, taking them two at a time and entirely avoiding the broken tread.

For a week, Beth insisted on listening to Louise. She would put Ethan to sleep in Michael's old room, then come to the basement, curl up in Will's easy chair and fasten her gaze on the radio with a television watcher's intensity. Her reactions confused Will. If she thought something Louise said was funny, she'd frown and cry out, "No way!" If Louise said something frankly cruel, Beth would laugh with robust glee. Will began to think of Beth as a machine that was missing some important bolt or screw. He imagined taking her apart, laying all the pieces on the floor, then putting her back together the right way.

"She's fat," Beth declared one evening, when there was a lull in Louise's calls. "She's got a fat kind of voice. Like it takes a lot of breath to get anything up and out."

"Oh, I don't think so."

"Yeah," Beth said. "She is. I'm sure about it."

He was offended and did not want to continue the conversation. Since Michael's death, Will's body resisted sleep and he used his fantasies about Louise to coax himself to orgasms which relaxed him. He often imagined that she was in her early thirties, with long red hair that fell alluringly between heavy, freckled breasts. At other times, he imagined her dark, and perhaps a smoker from the way her voice cracked when it rose to a certain register. Many times she had no face at all, only a round and pliant body, seen from behind.

"She's thirty-five, maybe older," Beth said. "Things are starting to get hairy in the biological clock department, so she has to make up these stories. Because she knows they'll never happen."

"I don't picture her the way you do," Will said, trying to appear neutral. "I picture her thin."

"Maybe," she replied, unconvinced.

"A heavy girl with no looks?" he said. "I don't think she'd get this many calls."

"There's somebody in this world for everybody," Beth said, rising to go. "Except for you and me. We're stuck listening to a radio."

Later that night, Will lay awake in bed. He tried to imagine Louise, but could not because now she was too many opposing things: fat and thin, old and young, pitiful and brave. Rising, he walked down the hall towards the bathroom. The door to Michael's old room was ajar. In the hall light, he saw that Beth was sleeping, while the baby, nestled in her arm, sucked on an exposed breast. Will's momentary arousal was replaced by sadness as he remembered watching his wife nurse his son.

He returned to his room, more agitated than before. He wanted Beth to leave. He would force the lie out of her. She was using him for his money and his hospitality, but there was no more connection between them than any two strangers might have. Once her subterfuge was exposed, she would have to go.

The next morning, he rose early and waited at the kitchen table. She entered a half hour later with Ethan balanced on her hip. She bit one of the boy's tiny fingernails off with her teeth.

"Listen," he said. "You need to get a job. You have to start putting something away for the future."

Her eyes glassed over. "You said we could stay here as long as we liked."

"I know," he stumbled, losing his resolve. "It's just that—"

"Look," she interrupted, her voice hardening. "I don't want to be here, if that's what you think. We need a place to stay for a while with no rent until I figure out how I'm going to do this thing. You think we're here to sponge off you?"

"No," he said weakly.

"Ethan needs things. It's not fair to make him suffer."

The baby whimpered, then cried. Casting an accusatory look at Will, Beth began gently bouncing, trying to cajole the boy out of his tears. When Ethan settled, she held him out to Will.

"Take him," she demanded. "I need caffeine before I pass out."

Will took the child, surprised, as always, by Ethan's lightness—he was no heavier than a bundle of kindling. Will transferred the baby onto his shoulder, but his movement was so big that Ethan nearly fell down his back. Will tried cradling the baby, but Ethan began to whimper. Finally, Will held him to his chest in an awkward embrace. The baby's discomfort was made obvious by the renewed vigor of his cries.

"Walk him around a little," Beth said, testing her hot coffee with mincing sips. "He likes to move."

Will paced back and forth across the kitchen, keenly aware of Beth's gaze, and the fact that he was not succeeding with the child. He worried too that he might catch his foot on a chair leg, trip, and drop Ethan the way he'd once dropped Michael years ago. They had been at a gas station in the desert. One moment, Will had been holding his son, watching while the attendant wiped the windows clean with two perfect strokes of the squeegee. The next thing Will knew, the baby was lying on the pavement. He was helpless to explain what had happened. Michael hadn't squirmed free, and nothing had diverted Will's attention. Michael had simply fallen. Will and his wife had checked the baby for bruises and breaks, staring into his small pupils to determine if they were still of equal size. Michael cried for a time, then stopped, and, once Will and his wife determined that no damage had been done, they drove back to town. During the next few weeks, Will could not shake the image of his son lying on the hard ground. He replayed the scene, searching for some cause and berating himself for his carelessness. Years afterward, he would catch himself studying Michael's behavior for signs that the fall had, in fact, done harm. When Michael was at the peak of his rebellion, Will often believed that his mistake was at the root of the problem, and that the astonishing disappearance of his sweetly compliant son could be related to that spring morning, when Will had simply let the boy go.

In Will's arms, Ethan's cries grew stronger. Will could not remember Michael being such a difficult baby. This thought only fueled his suspicion that Ethan was not his grandchild at all, and that he was being conned.

"Take your son," he demanded, holding the child out in the air. "I don't know what's wrong with him."

"He's a baby."

"Well, I've never seen a baby act like this."

Beth smiled. "Now you know what it feels like when the doctor hands you a screaming kid and says, 'Here, take care of him for the rest of his life.'"

Will's rental shop sat on Lankersheim between a BMW dealership and a tire shop. Forty years ago, when Will had first bought the franchise, he could see clear across Toluca Lake to the mountains without buildings obstructing his view. On a slow day, he'd take a drive to the foothills and watch the horseback riders negotiate the trails. Occasionally a deer or a coyote would lose its way and end up in the middle of Barham Boulevard, trotting alongside the cars, until it found its way back into the thicket.

Business had picked up in the last five years, due to a healthy economy and the do-it-yourself home improvement programs on TV. By two in the afternoon, Will had handled four rentals and the return of a circular saw. He was cleaning off the machine and oiling it when the bell above the front door jingled again. He looked up to see Beth. She carried an infant car seat awkwardly on one arm, banging it against the door as she entered. The day was hot. Her face was flushed, giving her a fresh and pretty look. She placed the carrier on the floor, walked up to Will's counter, and slapped a small blue bank savings book down.

"I got a job starting tomorrow."

"A job? So fast?" he asked, failing to hide his disbelief.

"I'm not entirely useless. The pay is low, but I can keep Ethan with me, so I save on day care as long as he stays quiet." She picked up the passbook and waved it in front of Will. "We'll be out of your hair before you know it."

When Will did not respond, she clicked her tongue. "Jesus, I thought you'd be jumping up and down for joy."

"What kind of a job is it?"

"Flower shop in the mall. I do bouquets."

The thought of her arranging anything of beauty struck Will as unlikely. "Is this work you've had experience in?" he asked.

"You think I'm lying. You don't believe I have the job."

"Of course I do."

"I took a test, all right?" she snapped, ignoring him. "I did a wedding number out of four kinds of flowers. The guy who owns the shop said my arrangement had flair."

"Well," Will said carefully. "Very good."

"You're like my old math teacher, Mrs. Stockton, you know that?" she said. "I could get nine out of ten right and she'd be going on about the one I missed." She picked up the sleeping baby in his carrier and walked towards the door. "Hey," she said, turning back towards him. "Did you know you could open a savings account with one dollar?" She stared at the passbook, marveling at her discovery, then turned and left the store.

As Will watched her disappear into the white light outside the doors, a hollowness settled over him. He felt the same emptiness he'd experienced those first few months after Michael's death. Then, his solitude had ceased to offer him comfort, but only filled him with a dread that lurked like thickening air before a storm. He had done anything to avoid staying home: working late, accepting invitations from concerned friends he had not seen since his wife's funeral. He had even visited a massage parlor in Koreatown, but the pleasure he received there did not last beyond the walls of the establishment. It had taken months for him to find solace, once again, in his isolation.

Will calculated quickly in his head. Even with minimum wage, Beth had no expenses and could begin saving quickly. In a matter of months, she'd have enough to put down for an apartment of her own up north, in the small town where she and Michael had lived.

The following day, he closed his shop early, then drove to the mall in Sherman Oaks where Beth worked. He wanted to make sure she was telling the truth about her job. If she was, perhaps he would buy a bouquet and help her prove that she was a valuable employee.

The mall was enormous. Its shopping spokes reached in four separate directions and it took Will nearly half an hour to locate Beth. Her flower store turned out to be a free-standing cart located in the wide avenue separating the mall shops. Buckets containing loose flowers were spread out around the cart, along with a few prearranged bouquets. Balloons printed with birthday and "Get Well Soon" messages floated above the cart, swaying gently back and forth in the air-conditioning vent wind. There were no customers. Beth sat on a stool, idly wheeling Ethan's stroller back and forth, while a somewhat older man, wearing a tan leather blazer and pressed blue jeans, busied himself with some of the flowers. Will assumed this was her boss. Will hid behind a fountain that boasted a trickle of water falling on plastic plants with fronds as big as surfboards. From there, he watched Beth, fairly certain she could not see him. Two teenage girls with exposed bellies walked up to the stall, fingered some stems, then left without a purchase. Beth took Ethan out of the stroller and walked him up and down near the cart. An older woman approached, and the boss gestured to Beth, who lay Ethan down, then collected a bouquet of yellow and pink flowers at the customer's direction. Will watched as Beth arranged the stems, clipped them, surrounded them with greens, and finally wrapped them in paper. His body shifted along with her movements, silently coaching her. He let out his breath only when the transaction was completed. He watched for fifteen minutes more, until Beth and her boss began to collect the buckets and close up the cart. Then he left the mall quickly, before Beth had a chance to see him.

For the next week, he closed the rental shop early and took his post behind the fountain. He knew he was being reckless, missing valuable end-of-the-day business. But he had become engrossed in the minor dramas unfolding at Beth's flower stall and he could not stop himself from returning each day. He took pleasure in Beth's apparent success with customers, was slightly bothered by the congenial relationship she was developing with her boss, and worried when she had to step more than a few paces from the stroller to complete a transaction. Once, when she had taken Ethan and disappeared for over ten minutes, Will almost flagged down a security guard to search for her. But before he could, she returned, and he realized she must have simply gone on a break, or perhaps found a private place to nurse the baby.

Upon Beth's arrival in Los Angeles, Will had found her confounding in an irksome and uninteresting way. Now, he became obsessed with finding out everything he could about her. At home, after she had left for the mall in her Toyota, and on the afternoons when he was the first to return home, he went to her bedroom. He looked in her closet, where her flannel shirts and worn blue jeans hung below the boxes of Michael's childhood memorabilia. He noted how few clothes she owned, and how ill-kept they were, shirts hung inside out and shrugging unevenly off hangers, pants folded against their seams. On Michael's old desk, he discovered pots of makeup and unscrewed the tops, inhaling the candy odor of the pink and red creams. Nearby, a white cardboard jeweler's box held a gold chain. A skull and crossbones hung off it, along with a tarnished silver cross bearing the delicately sculpted body of Christ. On the bed, he found a half-empty packet of colorful Chiclets chewing gum, and Michael's children's version of *Gulliver's Travels*, her place saved with a worn toothbrush.

As Beth's job continued, she became more pleasant at home. Will began to look forward to dinner, when she would recount the events of the day, telling him how she got the upper hand with an annoying customer, or retelling a joke that Ron, her boss, had told her. In the evenings, Will would catch her alone, looking at the pages of her bankbook and moving her lips silently as she tallied up her savings.

One Friday, she arrived home in a particularly good mood, her arms full of Ethan and the remaindered flowers of the week. "Freebies," she announced, laying the stems on the kitchen table. "They'll die before the weekend is out, so Ron gave them to me."

"He's generous," Will said.

"He better be. We're going out for drinks tonight and I'm sure as hell not paying." She blushed and smiled down at her feet. "I'll put Ethan to bed before I go and I'll be back before his midnight feeding. You won't have to do a thing." Without waiting for Will to agree, she carried the baby upstairs. "Mommy's going on an eenie-weenie date!" she said as she climbed. "Ain't that a trip?"

The idea of caring for the child made Will nervous. He started to move towards the stairs to protest, but she'd already turned on the shower.

At eight forty-five, she appeared in the kitchen holding a baby bottle full of milk, which she put into the refrigerator. She wore a short skirt which was nearly hidden by an over-sized flannel shirt. Her legs were bare and it appeared she was wearing no socks in her work boots. Two Band-Aids were stretched across each kneecap.

"I get impatient," she said, noticing Will looking at her knees. "It looks stupid, right?"

"Just like it might have hurt, that's all."

"What do I care, anyway?" she said. "It's not like I'm looking to get laid." She twisted a strand of hair nervously between her thumb and forefinger. "Let's just hope he's not a complete psycho."

"You'll have a good time," he said, his voice catching awkwardly in his throat.

"I doubt it," she said. She put on her jean jacket, then reached inside the sleeves to yank down the bulky arms of her shirt. "He's asleep," she said, gesturing up with her head. "You'll be okay with him?"

"We'll do fine."

"I pumped a few ounces for him if he gets up. You know how to heat it?"

"I remember."

"Warm, not hot. Test it on your wrist. And check him once in a while too, okay? Make sure he's still breathing." She sighed audibly. "For the entire time he's been alive, I've never been away from him. Isn't that freaky?" Will thought she was about to cry, but her attention shifted abruptly when headlights from a car shone through the kitchen window and moved across the room. When the horn sounded, she drew in a sharp breath.

"Romeo's here," she said, and marched through the kitchen door.

Standing at the window, Will watched as she trotted towards the twin cones of swirling light, pulling her jacket around her

with her small hands as she ran. Her pale legs shone against the
darkness. Will felt as though he had forgotten to tell her something important, some warning or wisdom, but by the time
the car drove out of the driveway, he still had not thought of
what it might be.

He hadn't been alone in his house a single night since
Beth's arrival and he looked forward to uninterrupted time
with his shortwave. Climbing downstairs, he turned on the
radio, tuning in to the North Hollywood Police Precinct. He
listened for a while, trying to decipher the dispatcher's lingo,
but became quickly bored and began searching for Louise's
line. He toggled the dial back and forth, but he could not find
her. Leaving the radio turned on, he went to check on the
baby.

Ethan lay on his back in the center of Michael's old bed,
surrounded by a makeshift bumper of pillows. His arms were
flung on either side of him and his fingers curled gently as if
he were waiting for silver dollars to be dropped into his palms.
Watching the baby breathe, Will thought appreciatively of how
flawless a machine the body was, but when Ethan seemed to
skip a breath, Will was overcome by how easily everything
could go wrong. Suddenly, as if aware of Will's thoughts,
Ethan let out a piercing scream and his eyes snapped open in
fright. Will scooped the boy up and cradled him in his arms,
but Ethan cried louder still. Taking the baby into the hallway,
Will paced back and forth without result. The cries racked
Ethan's small body. His arms and legs stiffened and thrashed
against Will, who was startled by the combined strength of the
boy's need and rejection.

The baby's cries finally subsided into short, desperate gulps. Ethan turned his small head towards Will's chest, his fishlike lips searching for a nipple. Carefully, Will carried the baby down-stairs and into the kitchen, where he found the bottle in the refrigerator. Still holding the child, he took a pot out of a low cabinet, filled it with an inch of water, and heated the milk. While he waited, he bounced and whispered to the increasingly agitated baby. When the water boiled, he turned off the flame, lifted the bottle and shook a few drops of the liquid onto his wrist. He absentmindedly licked the wetness that had run down over his palm, realizing, too late, that the milk in the bottle was Beth's. He had tasted something from her body. He rubbed his wrist against his pants, feeling as though he had done something perverse, a thing much more intimate than he could imagine having the courage to suggest or even knowingly desire.

Ethan sucked desperately at the bottle while reaching for Will's nose and cheeks with his hand. To Will's dismay, the feeding seemed to wake Ethan further and when the bottle was finally drained, the baby looked up at Will eagerly. Remembering a game Michael had once enjoyed, Will col-lected an armful of toys from the living room, then carried them and the baby up the stairs. He sat on the landing and propped Ethan in his lap, then began to pitch the toys down the stairway, one at a time.

"Heave ho!" he called softly, remembering the warlike cries Michael had uttered as he watched his toy soldiers fly through the air. Will hurled a stuffed bear along a graceful downward arc. "Gangway!" Will was pleased that Ethan was transfixed by the movement. He threw a soft rattle, which made a tinkling sound as it bumped across a carpeted tread. Next, he picked up a Raggedy Andy doll, waved its floppy form in front of Ethan's face, then sent it careening downward. He watched as the doll's flaccid arms and legs flopped and its cherry-red yarn hair blew in the tiny wind created by the fall. Like a surprise attack, the image of his son's falling body invaded Will's mind. He saw Michael's lean, muscular form rendered suddenly useless. Will's own face grew tight, his muscles struggling against the distortion that was now inevitable. Finally, warm tears ran down each cheek, onto his chin and the top of Ethan's head. Will hugged the baby to him, rocking back and forth until he could no longer feel Ethan move. The boy had fallen asleep in the warm cocoon of Will's embrace.

Exhausted, Will put Ethan back in bed, surrounding him with the protective pillows. Once downstairs, he collected the toys and was placing them back in the living room when he heard a voice coming from the basement.

"Come on over, please?" Louise pleaded, her voice crackling with static.

Will stood at the top of the basement stairs, listening.

"We could have a good time, baby. You know we could."

Will felt disgusted as he heard Louise's plaintive whine. Beth had been right: Louise was pathetic, begging for a little bit of romance she'd likely never get. He hurried down the stairs to turn off the radio. When he landed heavily on the broken tread, it snapped in two and he dropped sharply. His left leg sliced down into the cavern underneath the stairwell, the splintered wood scraping against his shin and thigh. He tried to break his fall, but his arm buckled beneath him.

"Please," Louise whimpered, "just give me a chance. . . . "

A stinging pain radiated from his wrist to his shoulder. Looking down, he could see that his leg was badly cut. He tried to use his one good arm to hoist his body up, but it was no use. He was trapped. The baby lay upstairs, only a cry away from needing his help.

"Is this how you treat all your girls?" Louise said sharply. "You get them into bed and do whatever you want, and then you just kiss them off?"

With all his remaining strength, Will reached for a piece of broken wood, wrenched it loose from its nail, and hurled it towards the radio. He missed and the wood clattered to the floor. Will's pain was so acute that he had to bite down on his shirtsleeve to keep himself from crying out and waking Ethan.

Louise was off the line by the time he heard the kitchen door open. Will listened as the metal buttons of Beth's jacket scraped against the Formica tabletop, and as the refrigerator door opened and closed with its customary hum. Will knew he should call to Beth, but he didn't want to see the look in her eyes when she realized how he had failed her. Her boots thumped upstairs, the sound growing faint as she headed down the hallway. He waited, imagining her movements: she would look in on the baby, then notice Will's wide-open bedroom door and the lights he had left on. . . . "Will?" she said, softly, casually. Then he heard her heavy footfalls running down the stairs. "Will?" she called more loudly, anxiety hardening her tone.

"I'm here," he said weakly.

"Will!" she cried out.

"I'm down here," he repeated, as strongly as he could. "Help me."

Beth surprised him with her efficiency. She climbed down the stairs carefully, assessing the situation before touching him. She argued that she should call the paramedics rather than move Will herself and risk a back injury, but he refused. Reluctantly, she let him have his way. Wrapping her arms around his stomach and bracing his back against her chest, she lodged one of her boots into the banister and pulled.

"You have to stop moving," she ordered. "You're resisting and it's making it ten times harder."

Her hands grasped for holds on his chest, his inner thighs, even his buttocks. Will submitted, helpless to do otherwise. Finally, she managed to lift him up enough so he could use his good leg and arm to get out of the hole. Embracing awkwardly, they climbed up to the landing.

Immediately she laid him down on his back. "Tell me when it hurts," she said quietly. She felt his groin, his chest, his face, his neck. It was not her intimacy but the lack of it that embarrassed Will. He was just a broken body that somebody would need to fix.

Two and a half weeks later, when the wounds on his leg had begun to heal and he had learned how to negotiate with his arm in a cast, Will held Ethan in his good arm while Beth folded clothes and put them in her suitcase. Will silently memorized the feel of the baby. He tried to place Ethan's smell. Was it sweet or clammy?

"If you send me your address, I can send money for him from time to time," he offered.

"You'd do that?" she asked, surprised.

"Of course. I'm his grandfather."

She looked at him strangely and, for a moment, he thought she might say the one thing that would separate them forever.

"If that's what you want," she said, shrugging. She turned back to her packing. Will kissed the top of Ethan's head. Dust. The boy's smell was as dry and familiar as dust.

GUNSMOKE

My father has a gun and won't come out of his house. This is what a policeman is telling me over the phone, a cop who used to be the boy I slept with in high school. I haven't seen or heard from Bobby in nearly twenty years, but a familiar stumble in his laugh reminds me of awkward silences relieved by fast sex.

Bobby keeps talking and, after a little more explanation, I learn that the bank has foreclosed on my father's house in the desert. Apparently, he failed to make his payments, so the bank turned around and sold his land to a real estate developer who's capitalizing on the fact that the desert is "back," as though it's been hiding out all this time.

"He hasn't shot anybody yet," Bobby continues. "But the chief's ready to escalate things."

"Meaning?"

"Throw some smoke in there and force him out."

"Jesus."

"I said, 'Let's give Alice a chance,' out of respect for your old man."

I try to imagine my father as a person who might inspire respect. He lives alone in the high desert, in the same flat-roofed cabin he's lived in since he left me and my mother when I was ten. He's taciturn to the point of being rude. He would not help out another person, not because he is selfish or mean, but because it makes him uncomfortable to be on the receiving end of gratitude.

Now Bobby tells me that he was made a sergeant on the force, and about somebody named Cindy and two kids.

"That's good news," I say, hardly listening. My gaze falls on my living room's single piece of decoration: an unframed poster of a Hong Kong action film I've never seen.

"It's nothing like your news, Alice," Bobby says. "We saw you on TV in that Greek thing."

I wince at the reference to a bit part in a superhero-of-the-ancient-world television show I guest starred on. "That was eight years ago."

"Everybody watched it. You ought to let us know when you're on TV more often."

"I'm not on TV more often."

"Well, you just let us know when you are."

Apparently he has not heard me. Or maybe it's that stubborn way people from back home have of ignoring cynicism. As it took me no time to discover, I'm no actress. In my seventeen years in Los Angeles, I have failed to create any illusion about myself whatsoever.

"You're doing movies now?" he asks.

"I do the voices in the background of movies."

"Oh," he says, uncertainly.

"You know all those people drowning in *Titanic*?"

"You were in *Titanic*?"

"I was the screams of some of the people drowning. Also, some of the eating sounds in the dining room scenes."

"Eating sounds?"

"I chew." I make some disgusting snicks and cheek-sucking sounds. I stop abruptly. "I do voice work," I say apologetically. "It's a pretty good job."

"I bet," he says optimistically.

There follows a long silence during which there is no movement in the air over the line.

"Listen, Alice. Are you going to get involved in this situation or not?" Bobby says. His voice has resumed its official staccato.

"I'll give him a call," I say.

"He's cut the phone lines. You'll have to come out here."

Last year, when I visited my father, we walked around his property while he pointed out some new fissures in the foundation caused by the latest earthquake. Then he spent forty-five minutes under the hood of my car, trying to fix a

fifteen-year-old engine cough. We drank a beer each for dinner. He said, "You don't have to come all the way out here,
Alice," and I said "It's no trouble at all." We said goodbye with
our hands stuffed in our pockets and I drove home. It felt like
the relief and disappointment of getting the same haircut over
and over again.

In the fifties and sixties, my father worked as a stuntman on
television westerns. His specialty was bulldogging—leaping
from one horse onto the back of another and wrestling its
rider to the ground. He once jumped from a moving train
onto a wagon, climbed down from the roof, knocked out the
driver, and drove the wagon down a steep hillside and across a
river. His range expanded until he could do almost anything—
take a fall off a saloon rooftop and land on a moving carriage,
dive from a cliff into a rushing river, ride underneath the belly
of a horse. He smelled of saddle leather and the tangy odor of
horse sweat.

In the early seventies he was involved in an accident. My
father and another man were supposed to get shot and fall off
a wooden watchtower. The tower was not especially high and
the stunt not a difficult one. Both men were experienced. My
father arrived at the set and arranged the crash pads. When the
time came to do the stunt, he made the fall first, tucking and
rolling himself to safety. But something went wrong when the
other man jumped. He fell and, instead of rolling onto the
landing rig, he bounced back up and slammed down on the
sharp rocks twenty yards away. He snapped his neck and died
instantaneously.

I grew up in Palm Springs. Up until the day before she died of a heart attack five years ago, my mother worked at many of the spas in the area, giving mud baths and heat treatments to rich tourists from L.A. and the Midwest. She wore white soft-soled nurse's shoes that made no sound when she walked. The first thing she'd do when she got home each night was take a bath in order to wash off the smells of other people. Then she'd crack open a head of lettuce on the edge of the kitchen counter and make our dinner.

The following morning I set out towards my father's house. As soon as I reach the outer edges of Riverside, life seems to give up and turn itself over to the desert. Car dealerships and mattress warehouses cluster together, desperate for company. Small communities rise up and just as quickly fall away. Billboards and fields of crops covered with tarpaulin take up the slack. The fact of the nothingness surrounding me makes what is here stand out in high relief. Endless miles of electrical cable hang like necklaces between mannequin-like stanchions. I drive the serpentine stretch of road that crosses over a pass and when I am on the other side, wind turbines appear by the hundreds, an army of giant white pinwheels rotating slowly on tall stems. It's hard to imagine that their bovine motion does much to provide electricity, but life thrives in a desert with the least bit of sustenance.

I head off the main highway towards the town of Twenty-nine Palms, then begin the drive up into the high desert. I pass a gas station and a convenience store, trailer homes and low ranch houses scattered randomly, as though planted by a gardener throwing the *I Ching*. Farther on, the area is mostly populated by a rough carpet of cholla cactus and spidery ocotillos. Joshua trees begin to appear, their thick branches extending up towards the sky and ending in spiky mittens of leaves.

A police cruiser is parked in the dirt driveway of my father's cabin. The scene is less dramatic than the bad TV movie I expected. Two cops sit in the car. One reads a newspaper while the other sleeps, head tilted back against the headrest. I start towards the cabin when the cruiser door swings open and out steps a barely recognizable Bobby, rubbing his eyes. His long half-miler's body has filled out with heavy muscles and the slightest hint of a gut. His uniform grips him.

"Can I help you?" he asks.

"It's me. Alice."

He comes a few steps closer and squints into the winter sun. "I didn't recognize you," he says. I detect the letdown in his voice. After my decade in the fast lane, he expects something more than a weather-beaten woman in jeans and a wrinkled blouse.

"It's been a long time," I say.

He nods. His face has grown more angular with age. His eyes have narrowed, as if they have been looking too long at difficult things. His lips fall into a natural pout, an attribute I found irresistible when I was young. I remember his tongue bursting inside my mouth with its tastes of ham-and-cheese sandwich and sweet cigarette breath. I remember, too, his eyes sleepy with desire. I feel a perverse and embarrassing connection to this stranger, as though the mere sight of him has snagged up my past like a fishhook and brought it hurtling into my present.

"Does he know I'm coming?" I say.

"He won't communicate with us."

I start for the kitchen door, but Bobby moves to block my path.

"I'm going to have to search you before you go in."

"You're kidding."

"Policy."

"You asked me to come out here, Bobby."

"The situation is, we've got a man in there with a gun," he says, resting his hand gently on his holster.

"There's a lot of people out here with a gun in their house."

He gives me an unfriendly look and I spread my legs and arms. He squats as he makes his way down my body, gingerly avoiding my breasts but not my inner thighs. His light brown hair speckled with gray glistens like sweat.

"This is a perk of the job, I guess," I joke uncomfortably. He doesn't answer. I look out beyond the top of his head at the lot across the street where the armature of an oversized hacienda-to-be stands like a mastodon skeleton.

"All right," he says, standing up. "See what you can do. The guy who bought the land is on our butt every day."

I take a step towards the house when a window flies open and the barrel of a shotgun slides out. Bobby dives behind the car, leaving me wide open.

"Dad?" I yell sharply. "Dad, it's me! Don't shoot."

———

Most people don't age well. Desert rats do it the worst. I meet my father in the kitchen and he looks more gecko than man. At sixty-eight, his hair is fully gray and age spots dot his high forehead like dollops of chocolate. His skin looks like it's about to peel off in big leathery plates. He's got a cowboy's build: compact and wiry, hips narrower than my own. A small shark could swim through his bowed legs. He studies me with eyes as bright as blue crystals.

"You usually call before you visit," he says.

"You usually have a phone."

"The police tell you to come get me out of my house?"

"I guess it isn't your house anymore."

We're both silent for a long time, as if we've expended all the words we know how to say to one another.

I look around the small kitchen. The counters are bare except for a set of aluminum canisters that descend in size. One says "Coffee," another "Tea." The letters are scratched off the other two. A blue-and-white striped dish towel hangs over the oven handle. A clock in the shape of a daisy is nailed to the wall. It's been almost a year since I've been here. Nothing has changed.

"How are you, Dad?" I say finally. He meets my gaze directly.

"How does it look?"

"You have some boxes somewhere?" I say, ignoring him. "I'll help you start packing."

I move a step towards him and he shifts his gun in his hands purposefully.

"Dad?" I say weakly. He doesn't look crazy, just determined.

"I'm not interested in help, if that's all right with you, Alice."

"Okay," I say. "Just put the gun down, will you?"

He lowers it to his side. We stand without speaking, avoiding looking at one another.

"You hungry?" he says finally.

"What?"

"I'll open up a couple of cans."

He sets his gun against the kitchen chair, opens a cupboard, and takes down two medium-sized cans. He routs around in a drawer, finds the opener, and sets to work.

"Soup okay with you?" he asks with his back to me. "I've run out of everything else."

I stare at the gun lying there for the taking and consider my options. "Soup's fine," I say.

When he was a young man, barely in his twenties, my father came south from Grass Valley. He'd been working ranches since he was sixteen and heard there was work down in L.A. for men like him. He was good-looking and could handle a horse in any situation and, once he landed his first job, the work came easily. Occasionally, I'll tune into a late-night rerun and catch a glimpse of him when he was a young man. In one battle scene between the Indians and the army, he played on both sides, dressing as a Comanche for one set of shots, then changing into a lieutenant's uniform for the other. When they put together the show, there was a scene of a heavily made-up Indian pulling a soldier off a horse. The Indian stabbed the soldier in the chest with a knife at close range. The final two close-ups of the victor and the vanquished revealed them to be the same man.

Once my father overheard me bragging to a playmate about how brave my Dad was. When the friend had gone home, my father sat me down and explained to me that he was not brave. The job, he said, was all about calculations. How fast was the horse going? How far did you have to jump? What was the wind going to do to your rate of spin? Once you made those computations, he said, the rest of it was being able to change on a dime. "What if the horse gets up too much speed?" he said. "What if she gets spooked by the camera car and turns to the left when I need her to go right? How do I react?" He told me that, in the end, things will happen you could never be prepared for. You just had to be ready.

"Bravery will get you killed," he said.

"I'm sorry," I said, ashamed of my exuberance and my love for him.

He looked at me uncomfortably. "You ought not to go on about things like you do, Alice," he said.

My father's living room is decorated with cast-offs from television shows. There's a rocking chair made out of rough-hewn bent wood, a couch with antlers where a headrest should be. A wooden wine barrel shot through with bullet holes from a bar fight serves as a coffee table. There are pictures of cowboys and horses on the walls, but they are cheap dime-store reproductions and have nothing to do with my father personally.

The shades are drawn against the glare of the afternoon sun

and maybe the police as well. My father sits in his chair in the dim light cast by a standing lamp. His shotgun lies across his lap.

"The house looks good," I say.

"Started sinking about a year ago. Drainage problem. I had to pour in a new foundation."

"That's a big job."

"I did the work myself."

We fall back into silence.

"I hit some traffic on the way out," I say finally.

"Umm?"

"There was a snarl downtown where the five meets the one-ten, but after that things cleared up."

"That's a bad interchange. Always has been."

"Yes."

Outside the police car starts up. I feel as grateful for the interruption as if an old friend had suddenly entered the room. I stand at the window and lift the curtain. The car pulls out of the driveway and heads down the road.

"You can probably find a reasonable apartment in Palm Springs or Indio," I say, sitting down on the couch. The antlers poke into the back of my head. "You must have retirement benefits from the union."

He sighs heavily.

"I could make some calls for you."

"Phone's dead."

"Would you like me to make some calls for you, Dad?"

"Not really."

When I was nine and my father was still living at home, my mother suggested he take me to work with him. She thought it would be a good way for us to spend time together. She picked out a day when I had no school. Normally, I would have accompanied her to a spa and sat on a hard stool outside the massage rooms reading Archie comics and eating a bag of potato chips from the vending machine. I'd watch people come in wearing white robes and towel turbans on their heads. They would come back out a half hour or an hour later, flushed red and wobbling like Jell-O. The morning I was to accompany my father, she woke me hours before dawn. My cold nipples pressed against my undershirt. By the time I was down in the kitchen, my father was already in his jacket and was tossing his car keys impatiently from one hand to another.

We drove for nearly two hours in the dark. When my father turned off the highway, the sun was just beginning to lighten the sky to a dove gray. I could tell we weren't in the desert anymore because there were too many of the wrong kind of trees. Finally, we pulled off the road and parked in a dirt lot filled with cars and trailers. My father grabbed a wrinkled brown grocery sack from the back seat and motioned for me to get out of the car.

I followed my father through a maze of trucks to a trailer filled with racks of clothing. A woman stood inside wearing a red sweatshirt. Dime-store bifocals hung on a chain over her heavy chest.

"You're a full head shorter than your actor," she said, looking my father over. "But I guess it doesn't matter, if you're on a horse."

She pawed through the clothes and came up with a pair of dusty brown pants and a checked shirt. "We only have doubles, so save the blood for the money shots." She handed him a hat and some brown suede chaps. "You bring your own boots?"

He held up his paper sack.

"I didn't see anything about kids on the call sheet today," she said, looking over a list on her clipboard.

"She's just a visitor," my father said, nudging me out the trailer door.

I waited outside a portable bathroom while he changed into his costume. My father emerged surrounded by a blast of urine and powerful disinfectant looking like a real cowboy. His chaps swung loosely around his legs. His hat sat back perfectly on his head. He carried his regular clothes and shoes in a bundle under his arm.

I followed him through the tangle of people drinking from Styrofoam cups of coffee. My father didn't stop to greet anyone. He led us to a horse trailer, found two wooden apple boxes, and told me to sit on one. The smell of hay and manure tickled my nose.

We sat on our boxes as the sun crawled higher in the sky. People continued to amble back and forth, some shouting orders into walkie-talkies. Men carried cameras and heavy cables off trucks and dragged them away on dollies. Everybody smoked. My father read a newspaper down to the advertisements for hair implants. He got up once or twice to straighten his outfit or to get himself another cup of coffee. The day heated up and he began to sweat under his hat, but he did not take it off.

Finally, a man wearing headphones beckoned impatiently to us. My father stood abruptly, adjusted his chaps and his shirt, and headed off after the man. I followed. We climbed a path rising up the side of a small hill. On the other side, people in western costumes sat in deck chairs, smoking, reading magazines, or talking to one another. My father motioned for me to stand out of the way and he continued on towards the people. I lost sight of him for a few minutes and when I saw him again, he was riding a horse. He was wearing a holster now and I could see the silver handle of a gun by his side. The horse was skittish and my father had to work to get it settled, but soon the horse's high, nervous steps fell under his control. He listened carefully while a man on the ground talked and pointed. Then he trotted the horse away behind a stand of trees. After a few more minutes, he rode out from behind the trees at full gallop. The crowd stopped talking and turned their attention to him. The horse reared up and my father slid off its back, doing a full flip and landing on his stomach on the ground. Immediately, people began to talk and move around as if nothing interesting had happened. My father got up, dusted himself off, and led his horse away a couple hundred feet. After another fifteen minutes, walkie-talkies echoed with the news that the filming was going to start. My father stood by his horse while a woman fluffed his hair. The lady from the costume trailer came over and fiddled with his pants legs and tucked his oversized shirt into the waist of his pants. It embarrassed me to see him touched so intrusively. When the women were finished fussing, he mounted his horse and disappeared behind the trees. An angry voice called "action" and my father rode in at a gallop again. Someone yelled "Gun!" and my father grabbed his chest. Blood poured out between his fingers as the horse reared up. My father flipped over and landed on his belly.

"Dad!" I screamed. I ran and knelt down beside him. Blood soaked the ground beneath his chest. I held his shoulders and shook him as hard as I could. I was crying.

"Cut!" someone yelled. "There's a kid in the shot! We have to go again!"

My father rolled over and sat up. He looked at me incredulously, then glanced up to see people staring at us. "Get back to where I told you," he hissed.

As I walked away, I passed a woman who smiled like she felt sorry for me. I heard laughter, but I was too ashamed to look up and see if it was aimed in my direction. When I got back to my spot, I looked for my father. He was being changed into a clean shirt by the wardrobe lady. He didn't look in my direction.

Later, I waited while he changed into his regular clothes and washed the fake blood off his hands in the portable bathroom sink.

My father is sleeping with his head tilted back against the chair. His mouth is opened slightly and I can hear the air pass through his throat like a dry wind. I'm thinking about old boyfriends to pass the time.

I was engaged once. We drove down to Baja to get married. When we stopped at the boarder checkpoint, this man placed a hand on my knee and asked me what I was thinking. I told him I was thinking about being in one of the cars going in the opposite direction.

"You still here?" my father says, surprising me. He sighs deeply and pulls himself up taller in his chair. He checks his watch.

I stand up and peer through a crack in the closed drapes.

"Are they back yet?" he asks.

"No."

"Long lunch."

I let go of the drapes and turn around. He looks me over.

"You acting anymore?" he says.

"Not much. I'm doing voice work, for the most part. Stunt talking."

He smiles at the joke. "I never thought you'd make a very good actor."

His comment rattles me. "I wish you'd have said something a couple of decades ago," I say, trying for a joke. "You could have saved me a lot of hassle."

"It wasn't for me to say what you should or shouldn't do with yourself."

"What made you think I'd be no good at it?"

He thinks for a moment. "Actors," he says finally, "need to be loved."

I feel as though I am standing in front of him with no clothes on. I turn around and peer out the window once more.

"What do you think's going to happen in this situation, Dad?" I say with my back to him.

"I have no idea."

"What's your next move?"

"To wait and see," he says.

I turn to him. The hair on the top of his head is thinning. His scalp is freckled and mapped with veins.

"Do you ever get lonely out here, Dad?"

He looks up at me with a confounded expression. I regret my questions. My stomach knots up at the thought of any kind of revelation.

"Not once," he says, reminding me that I'm a distraction.

The man who died in the accident my father was involved in was someone I knew. His name was Dan Radley. He was a stunt man like my father and he and my mother had an affair for a year before my father left. I was too young to know that at the time. I thought Dan came to help my mother out with heavy chores around the house during the time my father was away on television jobs. Dan wore a diamond as big as a gambling die on his pinkie finger. I admired the ring often and occasionally he would let me try it on.

Dan told jokes that he kept written down in a small black notebook. He'd fish the book out of his shirt pocket and call me over. "Why is six afraid of seven?" he'd ask, and before I could answer, he'd say, "Because seven eight nine. Get it?" He'd wink and give me a gentle pat on the bottom. When he told my mother a joke, they'd back away from me into another room. I'd hear her say "Oh, Dan. You're bad," like she was reprimanding him, but the pleasure in her voice was unmistak-able.

Dan was loud. The whole house filled up with the sound of him. He was from Canada originally, and he would tell us about the curling team standings, which he kept up with through relatives back in Edmonton. Sometimes we'd get a broom and a pot lid and play a game in the kitchen while my mother pretended to complain about her scuffed floors. Dan drank only imported beer. When he left our house after each visit, my mother would throw the bottles in the neighbor's trash.

When my father came home with the news of the accident, my mother collapsed to the floor. My father stood for a moment before going to her. Looking back on it, I don't know if he realized the situation right then, or if he had known for some time. He helped her up from the floor and steered her over to the couch, where she lay on her side with her knees to her chest and her back to us. He covered her with a crocheted blanket, filled a glass of water, and set it down on the table in front of the couch. Then he sat down on a chair and dropped his head into his hands.

"Something went wrong with the landing. He didn't have a chance to fix it," he said.

I burst into tears. My mother whimpered from the couch.

The family of Dan Radley sued the television company that produced the show. My father was named in the suit. A lawyer from the union came out to the house in Palm Springs to prepare him for his day in court. My mother and I stood in the doorway of the living room. My father sat in a chair, while the lawyer paced back and forth in front of him.

"Who came up with the stunt in question?" the man asked.

"Falling off the tower was in the script. Dan and I came up with how to do the jump."

"No," the lawyer interrupted. "You don't say that. You say the production company came up with the jump."

"The production company?" my father said. "They're some men in suits sitting in offices. What do they have to do with it?"

"They paid for the show," the lawyer said. "Everything that happened on the show is their responsibility. Who rigged the crash pad?"

"I did."

"No," the lawyer said impatiently. "That's not the right answer. The right answer is you did it according to the instructions of the movie production company."

"Every stuntman is responsible for his own pad," my father insisted. "I'm not going to go laying the blame on someone else."

"Don't use that word," the man said, growing heated. "No one is accusing you of rigging the pad wrong."

My father looked down. The man softened his tone.

"The crash pad worked fine for you," he said.

My father didn't respond. The man looked back at his papers.

"Can you describe for the court the way in which Mr. Radley took his fall?"

My father looked up at the man without speaking for a moment. "No," he said finally.

"No, you didn't see it?"

"I saw it."

"You have to answer the questions or you'll be held in contempt."

My father rubbed his chin with the heel of his hand. "A man ought to be able to die without people speaking poorly of him," he said finally.

My mother backed away from the door and disappeared down the hall.

After the accident, my father didn't work as much. At first he made excuses for turning down the jobs. Later, he just didn't answer the phone. The accident spooked him. He didn't trust himself on a job. Sometimes I would come home from school and catch him standing outside our house in Palm Springs, staring up at the roof. His lips would move but there was no sound coming from his mouth. His fingers would make calculations in the air. Some months later, he moved away from us, up into the high desert, exiling himself from the dual failures of his marriage and his job.

I'm driving in my car. I told my father I was going to the store to get something decent to eat. In truth, I don't know where I'm heading.

It's past five o'clock and the late winter sun is lowering. The distant mountain peaks glow a soft pink and then, a moment later, they darken. A tepid blue-gray color settles into the sky. A few miles down the highway, I pass Bobby in his civilian

SUV, headed in the opposite direction. We both slow as we pass. In my rearview mirror, I see that he has stopped his car. I do the same and wait as he expertly backs up the few hundred feet until he is alongside me. He's changed out of his uniform into jeans and a sweater.

"Back to the city?" he asks.

"To the store to make some phone calls. I'll try to find a place for him in Indio."

"If he's not out of there by tomorrow morning, we'll have to come in there and get him."

His tone irks me. "When did you become such an asshole?"

He doesn't look amused. "This is procedure. We could have your father in jail in one hour if you'd rather things went that way."

"Jesus, Bobby. With that kind of attitude you should be working for the L.A.P.D."

He finally cracks a smile. "There's a phone over at the Boot and Saddle."

"Where's that?"

"It's where I'm going." He accelerates and heads off.

At the bar, I call a few retirement complexes that are listed in the phone book, but it's nearly six o'clock and the offices are closed for the day. I hang up and head towards the bar where Bobby is seated next to an empty stool.

"Where's Cindy-two-kids?" I say, sliding in next to him and signaling for a beer.

"It's our night off."

"She's meeting you here?"

"Our night off from each other."

I look at the side of his face, trying to understand what he means.

He takes a drink of his beer. "It's her idea. She says we're in a rut, that we need to bring new experiences into the marriage. She joined a book group. She brings home books. I'm supposed to read them so we can have discussions."

"I don't remember you being much of a reader."

He smiles and looks at me. He studies my face in a way that makes me uncomfortable, as though he's measuring what I am against what I was.

"So you're bringing home your experiences in the bar?" I say. "That's your contribution?"

He doesn't smile. "She thinks I'm at the movies. I can't go home until ten-thirty or things will look bad."

"Doesn't she want to know what movie you've seen? For discussion purposes?"

"I check out the papers and see what's playing. You see who the stars are and what the ad looks like and you can pretty much get the gist of the story."

I laugh out loud. He shrugs, bashfully proud.

"Where are the kids?"

"They sleep over at her mother's. Cindy and I are supposed to, you know, get together when we come home." He looks down at his beer.

"Is that after the great books discussion or before?"

He shakes his head a little sadly.

"Well," I say. "Maybe she's right. Maybe things will perk up."

He takes a sip of his drink.

"Want to go to a movie?" he says. "Make an honest man out of me?"

This takes me by surprise and I laugh. Beer comes out my nose.

"That's nice, Alice. No wonder you can't find a husband."

"Fuck you, Bobby," I say lightly, trying to recover my dignity.

We grab a much-read paper from the end of the bar and scan the movie listings. We decide to drive all the way to Palm Springs in order to see a terrible teen flick I did voice work on a year ago but which is so bad it is only now being released. Bobby drives his car and I sit back with my window open, letting the cold night air slap me awake. The drive goes faster than I expect, and soon we're sneaking into the middle of the film, trying not to disturb the trickle of kids who've come out on a weeknight. I fill Bobby in on the plot, but it is so inane that soon the two of us are giggling into our popcorns and a couple of teenagers turn around in their seats and swear at us.

"Just tell me when you show up," Bobby whispers loudly.

"Not yet," I say. "There should be a party scene."

We watch some more. I glance over at Bobby, who's watching the screen with delight. A loud rock-and-roll song starts up on the soundtrack.

"The party scene!" Bobby whispers excitedly.

I watch carefully. "Okay, there!" I say, pointing as the camera lingers on a group of gossiping teenage girls. "I'm the voice of the blond."

"Where?" Bobby asks, sitting up.

"You missed it," I say, as the camera floats away from the

girls. "Okay, there, there!" I say, as the camera passes a girl and a boy laughing. "That's my laugh."

"That's your laugh! That's your laugh!" Bobby repeats, amazed.

"Okay, right here," I say, as the scene settles on the lead couple.

"That's you talking?" Bobby whispers.

"No. Wait. Just wait."

The couple leans in for a kiss. It is a wet, sloppy teenage kiss that goes on for a long time. "That's my kissing sound," I say.

"No way!" Bobby says, looking at me wide-eyed.

I nod, actually feeling proud. "Tongue sounds and everything."

Bobby looks back at the screen. He starts to yell. "Here's the girl who did the kiss. Here's the real movie star—"

I slap my hand over his mouth before he can go further, but he keeps trying to talk and his lips move against my palm. I'm laughing and he's struggling to get free of me so he can yell some more. Finally, he gives up and falls against the back of his seat. I start to take my hand away but he reaches up and holds it to his mouth. I feel the hot wet mist of his breath on my palm. His tongue licks my skin.

Within minutes, we're in his car, unbuckling and unsnapping, and then we're in a motel on top of an orange bedspread. My blouse is unbuttoned and my bra is pushed up over my breasts. One of Bobby's pant legs is still around his ankle. Neither one of us makes a noise or looks the other in the eyes.

He gives a final heave and falls into me with the whole weight of his body. He stays there for a long time, breathing heavily into the curve of my neck. I realize that we haven't even bothered to turn off the overhead light. There's trash in the opaque glass fixture. I raise my arm over my eyes to shield them from the lamp's glare.

I start to dread the moment that Bobby will lift himself up and we will see one another. I don't think I can tolerate the frankness or the need to make meaning out of what we've done. Bobby starts to move off me and I turn onto my stomach. I feel his weight move off the bed, hear the sound of clothing being pulled on, zipped up, the clack of a belt buckle. I think: don't talk, Bobby. Don't talk.

"Alice—"

I can hear the excuse already in his voice. I want to be past this moment before it has a chance to happen.

"Well," I say, turning onto my back and covering my eyes with my arms, "here's to bringing home new experiences."

I wake up on the antler couch in my father's living room. A blanket covers me although I have no memory of having gotten it or the pillow under my head. The insides of my thighs are raw.

My father is already in the kitchen, standing at the window. He holds the curtain open with the barrel of his gun. Outside, three cruisers are parked in the driveway. Cops crouch in positions behind their cars. I recognize the top of Bobby's head poking above an opened car door. A local television truck is parked further off. A man hoists a video camera onto his shoulder and points it at a well-dressed woman who begins speaking into her microphone.

A voice, squeezed and amplified by an electronic bullhorn, blasts through the walls of the cabin. "This is your final warning. Please vacate the house now!"

"They sent out the cavalry this time," my father says. He's watching carefully. His eyes scan the driveway, following the movements of the police. His body shifts back and forth, as if he is making minor adjustments to some plan in response to what he sees. His body is taut, ready to react. For the first time in years I feel frightened.

"Dad?"

"Yes, Alice."

"What happens to people like us?"

He turns to me. His face is stricken, as though he's lost his little girl in the park and is suddenly overcome by all the terrible possibilities. His mouth falls open as if he's about to say something, or apologize for something, but the sound of breaking glass startles us both. I rush to the living room where a gray canister lies on the rug. Smoke begins to hiss out of the can, twisting up around the windowsills. The oxygen gets sucked out of the room quickly and my lungs begin to hurt. I go back into the kitchen, holding the bottom of my blouse over my nose and mouth.

The smoke snakes its way into the kitchen. I try to say something, but I start coughing and double over. The air becomes thick. I stand up to look for my father, but I'm dizzy and can't get my bearings. I just barely make out the outline of the kitchen door. I head towards it, fumble for the knob, and fall outside onto the ground. I lie on my stomach for a moment, turning my head to the side, gasping for clean air.

Hands grab my arms, lift me and yank me away from the house. They push me towards a safe place behind a police car, then pull me down so that my head is well below the line of the car hood. I look to the side, where cops wearing clear protective masks crouch behind another vehicle. They are as still as statues until one of them turns towards me. Behind the wobbly glare of the mask, I see Bobby's face. It is impossible to make out his expression before he turns back in the direction of his weapon.

I hear the squawk of the bullhorn and someone shouts "He's coming out!" I lift myself so I can just see over the hood. The front door opens and the stooped shape of my father appears in the gray fog. Then all of a sudden people begin to shout in a panic.

"Gun!" someone calls, and I hear the snap of guns being cocked.

"Dad!" I call out, running towards him. When he sees me coming, he drops the gun to the ground and holds up his hands in surrender.

STATUES

The statues from the top of Janie and Peter's wedding cake rested on the windowsill of their tiny kitchen on Gower Street. Janie watched them every night as she washed the dishes, the warm soapy water collecting in the crooks of her elbows. The statues looked nothing like Janie or Peter. The woman was blond and buxom, her body ripe with expectation, the man sported a helmet of black, polished hair. His hands hung complacently by his sides. The plastic figures wore brilliant expressions that made them seem entitled to good fortune. Janie scrutinized herself in the window reflection. Her high forehead was distinctive and her features, when taken individually, were attractive. But altogether things didn't add up. People called her pretty, but she knew what they meant was that she certainly could not be considered ugly.

"We need to rent a house," Peter said. He sat at the yellow breakfast table behind Janie, tilting back against the wall on the unstable chair legs. Janie had found the table at a yard sale in Beachwood Canyon a year ago, when they had first moved to Los Angeles. She envisioned a breakfast nook in the kitchen where she and Peter could eat small, informal meals. Dinners would be eaten in the living room, on a larger, more solid table, just the way it had been in her family's home in Ohio. But all the dining room tables she'd seen were too expensive, so the kitchen table had to stand in for the bigger one, as well as for the other ideas she'd had about her life.

"We just can't live like this anymore," Peter continued, sighing as though they were at the tail end of an old argument. He rubbed the bridge of his nose where his eyeglasses had left sun-burned ovals, then raked his hand through his prematurely thinning hair.

"We can't live like what anymore?" Janie asked.

Lately, Peter had begun talking in pronouncements. "Casting that actor in the lead was a complete blunder," he'd say authoritatively, as they walked out of a movie theater. "That place is completely over," he'd declare as they drove past a watering hole they could never afford to be seen in. He seemed to be speaking recycled thoughts, ideas that had belonged to others before they ended up with him. Janie and Peter had once shared opinions on nearly everything. Together, they laughed about all the quirks of their new city— how you had to drive somewhere to take a walk, how complete strangers would write "clean me" in the dust on your car hood, or about the advertisement for a dog psychic that stood between the curtain and the window of the decrepit house across the street. But Janie had the feeling that Peter no longer found it funny when she'd comment on how a girl in her acting class had undergone yet *another* plastic surgery in order to fix a previously bungled one. And just the other day, when she noted how ridiculous it was that their neighbor paid a gardener to blow the leaves from his lawn onto theirs, Peter had seemed offended.

"People don't want debris all over their lawns," he'd argued. "It doesn't present a good image."

"But they're not accomplishing anything. It's like throwing dirty clothes under the bed."

Peter had looked at her sadly, as though he were gazing out the window of a moving passenger train as she stood on the platform, becoming tinier and harder to see.

Now, when he brought up the idea of a new house, she was careful. "Do you think we could find a whole house for what we can afford?"

"That's the thing," Peter said. "Maybe we should afford more."

"How?"

"This place is so small," Peter said, avoiding her question. "It's so . . . nothing."

Janie turned off the water. She turned to Peter, drying her hands on a dish towel. "Did your rich uncle just die or something?" she said. "Because last time I noticed, we were one paycheck away from my parents' basement in Akron."

Sometimes she had to remind herself that they were actually married and that this was not a TV show about a marriage. Everything about their lives seemed so temporary and fake, as though they were living on a movie set that was going to be dismantled the minute the tidy domestic scene was over. When they'd moved into the apartment, Janie's mother had sent a starter set of dishes. The four bowls and four dinner plates looked sad sitting all alone in the kitchen cabinet. When Janie used the dishes, the cabinet became alarmingly empty.

She turned back to drape the towel over the sink faucet. She picked up the wedding figurines. "Help! Help!" she cried, facing them towards the window and dancing them back and forth. "We're trapped and we can't get out!"

"That's weird," Peter said.

Janie replaced the statues, feeling foolish. Maybe Peter was right. Wasn't the whole point of marriage to keep trying to make things bigger? In the magazines she skimmed at the grocery store, people were always renovating or expanding, selling and buying, having babies, divorcing then remarrying, sometimes to the same people. Above all, everyone seemed to be having insights. Nonstop. Assaulting them like hailstorms. There seemed to be a goal, but the goal was to keep changing the goal. But whenever Janie tried to adopt this mind-set, she felt the way she did in acting class, when, right in the middle of a scene, she'd fall out of the moment like a bicycle chain disengaging from the gears. And then her teacher would look at her morosely and say, "Janie, where are you right now?"

"We were watching Leno at work last night," Peter said. He tended bar in Hollywood four nights a week so that he could have time during the day to write. "And this actress was on," he continued. "This famous actress, but I can't remember her name. She did a *Playboy* spread."

"Oh, great," Janie said. "And how do you know *that*?"

"Shut up," Peter said, smiling coyly. His dimples reminded her of how awkward and innocent he had been at college. He carried a novel with him wherever he went—to classes, parties, even football games. His height made him hunch. He kept his hands hidden in his pockets to disguise a small nervous tremor.

"I'm trying to make a point here," he continued.

"Which is?"

"Which is: she always *knew* she was going to be famous. I mean, even when she was just getting bimbo parts in B movies—"

"As opposed to A-list spreads in porno magazines."

"She's been in some really big movies. I just can't remember her name," Peter said, frustration beginning to crowd out his good humor. "Listen, will you let me make my point?"

"Sorry."

"My point is . . . " He paused, apparently forgetting his point. "That even before anybody would give her the time of day, she spent whatever money she had on really good clothes just so that she would have something to wear when she presented at the Oscars. Get it?"

"No." She had the feeling he was on that train again and that she'd have to cup her hands and yell to be heard.

"She didn't say *if* she presented at the Oscars. She said *when* she presented at the Oscars. She *knew* she was going to make it. And she's famous now. And last year she was a presenter at the Oscars." He slapped the table for emphasis.

"But you can't remember her name."

"That's not the point," he sighed.

Janie knew what the point was. Peter wanted her to be more savvy about L.A., to refer to it as *this town* as though she were on a nickname basis with it. But, frankly, Janie couldn't see much difference between the life they were living in L.A. and the one they might be living in Ohio. They had a tiny apartment on a block too close to Hollywood Boulevard to be safe. They made minimum wage working jobs they hated. They shared a car and worried about insurance payments. And at night, they ate off two of their four plates.

"It's pretty risky to bet your life savings on luck," Janie said.

"I just think," Peter said, his voice hardening with irritation, "that we should spend more in order to better our situation—"

"So that when our situation actually gets better, we'll have the right clothes on?"

"Right!" Peter said, relieved that Janie finally understood. "If we take ourselves seriously, other people will take us seriously too."

Janie imagined herself on the stage with a spotlight trained on the kitchen table. She tried to concentrate on how a girl like herself who was married to a boy like Peter should react in a moment like this. "Okay, honey," she said resolutely. "Let's look at a house."

He reached out his hand for her and she took it. In her mind, she heard the acting teacher clap his hands and yell

'Scene!' then turn to the group preparing to rip apart Janie and Peter's performance.

The next morning, Peter read through the rental listings in the *Times*. They discussed how much more than what they actually had they would be willing to spend. Gamely, Janie threw out one fictitious figure after another. She waited for one of her exaggerations to jolt Peter out of this delusional plan, but he considered her suggestions seriously.

At nine-thirty, she drove downtown to do accounting work for a manufacturer of hefty men's clothing, leaving Peter to make the calls and appointments. Later that day, when she returned home, Peter was waiting for her on the steps of their apartment house, holding a folded newspaper. He was wearing the striped shirt and navy trousers he'd bought for their wedding rehearsal dinner. He stood excitedly and motioned for her to pull up to the curb.

"We have an appointment," he said, climbing into the passenger seat. "It's in our price range."

"You mean the five hundred dollars a month more than we actually have?"

"Please, Janie. Just do this, okay?" He looked down at his red-inked real estate page. "'Hillside aerie. One-bedroom, pristine condition,'" he read, sounding like an overeager broker.

At least it was good to see him enthusiastic. His first screenplay, his thesis project, had won an award at college. The judge, an alumnus, was a Hollywood agent. He attached a note to

Peter's winning script encouraging Peter to "stay in touch."
That was enough to get Peter and Janie into the Volkswagen
along with their wedding money and everything they owned.
They followed a route that took them from Ohio, down
through Illinois, then across Kansas and Oklahoma, and eventually through the desert. Janie had been mesmerized by the
endlessness of the desert, with its spry cactus plants poking up
like exclamation points at the end of dull sentences. She was
intrigued by the outposts of windowless aluminum-sided
buildings that appeared out of nowhere. She thought there
must be bombs stored in these structures, or maybe secret
caches of radioactive waste. Her lurid imagination was spurred
on by the signs that appeared every so often along the highway warning, "No Food or Water for the Next 100 Miles."

Los Angeles, at first glance, seemed nothing like what Janie
had imagined it to be. She anticipated wide streets lined with
giraffe-necked palm trees, lawns as plush as carpets topped
with wide, complacent houses. She expected a kind of sheen
to bathe the city, as if glamour were a weather condition. But
all they could see from the freeway were the flat, dusty roofs of
sunstroked buildings, many of which were topped by billboards advertising refried beans and strip clubs. They passed
the downtown, which looked like downtown Cleveland or
Columbus. Old dilapidated buildings stood like embarrassed
wallflowers in the shadows of angular modern towers. But
rather than stopping in what seemed to be Los Angeles, the
highway signs said to keep going: Los Angeles lay still ahead.
Janie had a map, but this was no help because the city seemed
to be made up of many discreet parts, none of which was

exactly Los Angeles. Finally, Peter spotted the sign for the Hollywood Freeway. They were relieved. Now they could stop looking for Los Angeles, which seemed to be everywhere and nowhere at the same time.

But the freeway seemed to be without destination. It rambled on, past streets that had no significance for either Janie or Peter. Feeling hopeful, they exited the freeway at Hollywood Boulevard, but their enthusiasm diminished as they passed through the gaudy avenue filled with check-cashing stores and wig shops. They had all but given up when Janie looked up a side street and saw the tip of the Hollywood sign. Peter turned and drove up street after street, determined to get as close to this beacon as possible. Finally they drove up a dead-end street and stopped. Only the *H* and part of the *O* were visible from this vantage point. But a "For Rent" sign was planted in the grass in front of the unappealing apartment complex to their left, and they agreed that this was an omen. Their destinies lay somewhere in this unremarkable warren of streets and low stucco buildings. They rented the apartment that day.

Janie quickly found her accounting job, which enabled her to enroll in an acting class in North Hollywood in the evenings. Auditions would have to wait until she'd stockpiled some savings and could work part-time. Meanwhile, Peter contacted the agent who had been so encouraging to him, only to learn that the man had been fired. Discouraged, Peter moped around the apartment, making noises about packing up the car and driving back to Ohio. But Janie reminded him that they had signed a year's lease. During her acting class, she mentioned Peter's bad luck to another girl, who told Janie about a friend of hers who had a similar frustration but was now a famous writer with a house in Malibu.

Janie repeated the story to Peter and his outlook improved. Within a few days, he resolved to stick it out in L.A. Now he had written a pile of material. He sent the work to agents whose names he got from a book. After two months and no responses, he stopped writing altogether in order to devote all his time to learning "the business."

Learning the business consisted of reading the trade papers every day and spending a lot of time on the phone discussing the articles with other unemployed writers he knew. Sometimes Janie would overhear him saying things like "the budget is sixty-five mil below the line," or "he has a five-picture deal with points up front," and she would feel embarrassed, as though Peter had said something dirty.

Janie drove up Laurel Canyon Boulevard, then turned off on Lookout Mountain Drive. Peter was excited about the idea of living in the hills. At night, they often drove along Mulholland Drive, stopping to gaze down at the lights of the city spread out below like glowing pearls. Peter loved the feeling that so much was happening all the time, but the view made Janie feel the way she had as a child playing double Dutch. She'd count the rhythm to herself as the swingers waved the jump ropes in wide opposing arcs, certain that she knew the exact second to step in. But she always got tangled up in the ropes and no one had wanted her on their team.

She maneuvered the VW up the barely maintained street,

stopping intermittently to make way for cars coming in the opposite direction. These cars were always better-looking than theirs—BMWs or hulking sports utility vans that looked like they belonged in war—and Janie felt instinctively that it was up to her to yield the right-of-way. The same was true in acting class, where there were girls so mesmerizing that she found herself unconsciously making way for them. She'd give up her chair when they came into the full rehearsal room, or pass up her turn to run a scene so that one of them could take her place. These girls seemed to expect people to make such sacrifices and were never particularly grateful, which made Janie all the more certain she was doing the right thing. Janie was disarmed by the girls' beauty. It seemed almost impossible that eyes, nose, lips, and cheeks could all fall into place so perfectly. And their gestures—oh! They would lick their lips, or flick their hair, or drag a hand across their bare flat bellies with such insouciance. In their presence Janie felt like a cheerleader with as much mystery as banana bread.

As Peter read the map, Janie guided the car onto smaller and narrower unpaved roads until they found the one they were looking for. As the car bucked over ditches, Peter squinted past Janie to read the addresses. The street was lined with a hodgepodge of architecturally diffuse houses. A faux-tudor sat next to a modern box, which in turn sat beside a Kmart version of a French chateau.

"Here it is," Peter said, pointing to a pale pink house that seemed to make an aesthetic nod to a shoe box. Janie pulled over. Peter got out and crossed to the canyon side of the road and looked down into the bramble of brush and trees. "Isn't this great?" he exclaimed. "You'd never know you were in Los Angeles at all. I mean, it's a dirt road!"

"Maybe these people don't pay their taxes."

"This is what people want," Peter said. "It's a kind of Wild West thing. A kind of roughing-it thing."

Peter took her hand and eagerly crossed the road. He knocked on the thin wooden door. While they waited, he gave her hand a squeeze.

The woman who answered the door seemed to be two different people at once. Judging from her face, she looked to be forty-five or fifty. Her wrinkles were unsuccessfully camouflaged by heavy pancake makeup, petal-pink rouge, and blue eye shadow. From the neck down, however, she looked to be no more than twenty-five. She wore a unitard dance outfit which showed off muscled thighs, sinewy arms, and impossibly round breasts. Janie looked back and forth between the woman's face and her body, trying to get the discordant images to match up.

"We're here about the rental," Peter said. "I called earlier."

The woman stretched one arm so that she was holding on to the upper corner of the door, revealing a stubbly armpit. "This isn't the best time," she said, inhaling her words.

"Oh," Peter said, disappointed. "We had an appointment for six, didn't we?"

"I mean the light," the woman said. "Morning light makes everything look, you know, perkier."

"We could come back," Peter offered. "It's okay with us, right, honey?"

He put his arm around Janie's waist so that she was wedged uncomfortably against his side. They stood there for a moment, frozen in this awkward position, until Janie tugged at Peter's jacket, signaling that she wanted to leave. This double image of a woman, this flimsy door, the chipped gold-plated outdoor light fixture, hanging by an exposed wire over their heads, were all making her uneasy.

"Whatever works for you," Peter said, ignoring Janie. "We don't want to put you out."

"That's sweet," the woman said impassively. "Well, you're already here. You'll just have to use your . . . whatever. . . . " She walked back into the house, her hips swaying back and forth like a slow pendulum. Janie took a step backwards, but was pulled inside by the hopeful tug of Peter's hand.

The woman turned around and stood in the middle of the living room. She raised her arms on either side of her. "Ta-da," she sang, flatly.

The room was uninviting. The walls were painted lemon yellow, tinged by an overlay of dirt. There were cracks in the seams where the walls met each other. A water stain marked the ceiling like a burst of coffee-colored tie-dye. The deep blue shag carpet on the floor was old and balding in one discrete spot in the center. Janie could not imagine what might have gone on there to warrant the unfair wear and tear.

The furniture was not arranged in the usual way, inviting people to sit and look at one another. Rather, a red couch and two faded floral sitting chairs stood in a line, pushed up against one wall. In the corner by the window stood a home video camera on a tripod. Its lens tilted down to the floor as if the camera were nodding off.

Janie looked around the room for a family photograph or mementos of a trip, something familiar. On one wall she saw a group of horizontal pencil lines drawn one on top of the other.

"My mother used to do that," she said, hopefully. "Red for me, blue for my sister. I was always taller, even though I'm younger."

"Lucky you," the woman said. She gazed distractedly at the marks. "We had some boys here once."

Janie waited for a comforting discussion of children, but none came.

"Mia casa," the woman said dryly. "You don't want to see the rest, I guess."

The question was a challenge, as if other potential renters had fled before investigating further. The room was dingy, but that could be taken care of with a coat of paint. But the real problems were not cosmetic, they were more viral in nature. Janie had the impression that she and Peter would not inhabit this house but that the house would invade them.

"We'd love to!" Peter said.

Janie looked at him dumbfounded.

"And it has a yard too," Peter continued. He walked over to the sliding glass doors that looked out onto a patch of dirt studded with weeds. "Did you see this, honey?"

Janie met him by the windows. "Let's go," she whispered.

"You could plant things. And we could go hiking right out-side our front door."

"We had tomatoes once," the woman said, staring out the window as if she were looking at the faded pages of a photo album. "I don't even know where they came from. They were just there one day. Wild tomatoes or something."

"Can we see the bedroom?" Peter asked.

The woman didn't respond.

"We don't have to if it's a problem," Janie offered.

"No problemo," the woman said. "He won't care."

She led them to a door off the living room and opened it. Inside was a man sitting up in bed. He wore a pajama shirt, but the rest of him was hidden under layers of wrinkled blankets. Trumpets of curly gray hair sprang from his nearly bald head at unpredictable intervals, as though his pate were a garden he had failed to water properly. He was reading a hardcover book.

Janie gasped, as though they had walked in on someone going to the bathroom. She glanced at Peter, who looked uncertain.

"Take a look around," the woman said. "There's a walk-in closet the size of a goddamn basketball court in here. I don't know why."

Peter hung back for a second.

"Go on," the man urged. "It's really something."

Peter walked quickly past the bed and opened the closet. "Big," he said, barely peeking in before shutting the door. He looked back across the room at Janie as though he were stranded. Janie felt if she didn't do something, they'd be trapped in this room forever.

"I've always wanted a walk-in closet," she said hesitantly.

"Not that we need the space," the woman said. "I'll live and die in Spandex, if you know what I mean."

"That's her uniform," said the man without looking up from his book. "Nothing in her drawers but stretchy things."

Janie looked at the dresser where five identical gold statuettes sat on paper doilies.

"Look at those," Janie said, moving eagerly towards the dresser until she stood before the shapely golden figurines. "You've won a lot of awards."

"Oh, yes," the man said appreciatively. "Vivian's won so many."

"You must have been in a lot of movies," Janie said, turning to the woman. "Or did you work below the line?" She glanced at Peter, hoping he'd be proud of her lingo, but he only looked more desperate. "Peter and I are in the business too," Janie continued. "I mean, not like you. We're just starting out, really."

Janie turned back to the statues and leaned down to read the inscription on one of them. It read "Best Actress, Vivian Dawn," and below that, "Adult Film Awards, 1981."

"Oh," she said quietly, stepping away from the dresser.

"You watch many adult films?" the woman asked.

"Not really," Janie said quietly.

"That's what most people say," the man said.

"Is that why there's a camera in the living room?" Janie asked. "To make your films?"

"Oh, no, dear," the man said, laughing generously. "Although we did make one or two of our films right here in the house, right, Viv?"

"Not the good ones," the woman said.

He nodded. "Now we use the camera just for fun."

As the room fell into silence, Janie studied the woman more

closely. Her cheekbones were high. The hollows of the cheeks themselves were sunken like shadowed valleys. The lips were perfectly shaped, with a small hole in the center where the bottom lip met the top. The space made the woman seem as if she were on the verge of revealing a thought or holding in a secret. Despite the heavy makeup, the woman had the same inchoate beauty of the girls in acting class, an indescribable luster that caused her to shimmer more brightly than others around her, as if a candle burned beneath her skin.

Despite the woman's circumstances, Janie felt compelled by her. For the first time since coming to this incomprehensible city, she felt certain of her own desire. She wanted to be this woman—not the tawdry actress who stood before her, but the woman beneath that skin who was as impenetrable and mysterious as a star.

"Will you make a movie of me?" Janie said suddenly.

"Come on, Janie," Peter warned.

"Here? With your camera?" Janie asked the man. "Please?"

The man and the woman glanced at one another. "You'd have to pay for the blank tape," the woman said finally. "And the time."

"How much?" Janie said.

The woman looked Peter over, as if to assess his worth. "A hundred."

"Okay," Janie said, reaching into her purse. "Can I write you a check?"

"As long as you've got something to back it up," the woman said.

"Jesus, Janie," Peter said, crossing to her and grabbing her arm before she could retrieve her checkbook. He was frightened of her. She could see it in his eyes, feel it in his trembling hand.

"It's okay, honey," she said calmly, removing his grip from her arm. She found her checkbook and held it up. "Does anybody have a pen?"

Janie wrapped a bedsheet around her naked body while she waited for the man to set up the camera. By now the sun had gone down. The man searched underneath the sink and found a floodlight. He screwed it into one of the lamp sockets, took off the lampshade, and aimed it towards Janie. The light bounced off the yellow walls, giving the room a glow and obscuring the cracks and dirt and the mottled colors of the furniture.

"It's cold in here," Janie said, pulling her sheet more tightly around her.

"Cold's good," the woman said. "It makes your nipples hard."

Peter stood in the corner by the sliding glass doors. The woman moved past him, holding a bottle of makeup.

"Let me do something about those zits," she said, approaching Janie.

"Oh," Janie said, touching her face.

"On your bum, dear," the man said as he bent down to adjust the tripod. "Everybody has them, and believe me, nobody wants to see them."

Janie jumped as the woman bent down and lifted the sheet up around her hips. She tried not to move or laugh as the woman worked, painting the cold cream onto her ass with a makeup brush. She caught Peter's eye, but he looked away.

"That'll do it," the woman said, standing up and letting the sheet fall back down. She took an appraising look at Janie's face. "You're young," she said.

"Should I sit or stand?" Janie asked the woman.

"It's up to you. But a table can come in handy."

"Young fellow," the man said to Peter. "Could you be so kind?"

Peter winced and crossed to the dining table. Picking up one side, he dragged it over to where Janie stood. Then he retreated back to the corner by the windows.

"Perfect," the man said. "Now, what's your story going to be, dear?"

"I don't know," Janie said.

"It's a movie," the woman said. "You've got to have a story."

"I'm not very good at thinking of stories. Peter's the writer."

"Excellent," the man said, turning to Peter. "Writer, give us a script!"

Peter looked up, startled. His mouth dropped open, but no sound came out.

"Can you think of something?" Janie asked him.

"Something simple," the man added. "We don't want to get bogged down in too much complication. And of course we have no other actors. Unless you'd be willing to—"

"No!" Peter cried out.

The man shrugged and turned back to Janie. "I guess you'll have to improvise."

"I was never really good at that," Janie said. She shut her eyes and breathed deeply, just the way she had been taught in acting class before beginning a scene. Her head began to feel light and open as if she were an arid field, ready to be flooded with water. "Ready," she said, opening her eyes.

The man crouched down and put his eye to the lens. He pressed a button on the camera. "Action!"

She stared at the blank wall across from her. The streaks of dirt and rough paint began to take on life.

"Hello, darling," she purred. Her eyes roamed to the right, tracking the movements of her unseen visitor. "You wanted to see me?" she asked. "I knew that you did."

Even though the room was cold, she felt her body heating up. She put her hand on her cheek and felt the warmth there. She dragged her fingers lazily through her hair, lifting the strands languidly, as though the heat might be released through her scalp. She let the sheet fall slowly off her shoulders, revealing first her breasts, then her belly, then her crotch. Finally, the sheet fell to the floor, where it collected around her feet like a cloud. She felt the hot floodlight on her skin. She was in a desert. Someone was walking across the sand towards her. Her hand traced her shoulder, the swell of one breast, her thigh. She let it fall and graze over the rough island of hair between her legs. She held her other hand out before her, palm facing the stranger.

"Don't come any closer," she said. "Just look."

She lowered her arm and pushed herself onto the table. Lying down on her side, she draped her free arm across the V of her waist so that her hand lay against her gently sagging belly. Her breasts fell against one another, becoming more supple and shapely with their combined weight. She stayed in that position without moving. She could hear people breathing in the room around her and she knew they were looking at her. This man walking towards her in the desert was watching her too. They could see every inch of her, but they could not have her. She had them.

Peter drove them back down the hill in silence. He steered carefully so as to avoid hitting the cars parked for the night up along the side of the road. The videotape sat in the well between the seats, knocking against the hard plastic of the emergency brake handle. Peter turned the car onto Laurel Canyon Boulevard. Suddenly he swerved and pulled onto the shoulder. He got out and moved around the hood to the side of the road, where he doubled over and vomited.

When he got back into the car, Janie handed him a tissue from her purse. He took it and cleaned off his mouth, then stuffed the tissue into the ashtray. He started the car once more. He looked into his side mirror, anxiously judging the speed of the oncoming cars as they slid into view around the bend.

Janie twisted around and looked out the back window. She watched the cars rushing past, and looked for a break in the traffic. A pickup truck rumbled by, causing their car to vibrate in its wake. "Go right now!" she said.

He pulled into the narrow space between the truck and the next car and drove.

THE MISSING

In her seventieth year, Mariana's mother decided to take up public speaking. It was an unusual choice, given Dora's indecipherable accent; her own children often found it difficult to understand what she was saying. It was as though she had come over from Poland just the other day, rather than fifty-four years ago. Mariana and her brother Julian shared in their exasperation that Dora could be stubborn enough to resist proper English pronunciation. This recalcitrance stood, in their minds, for the aggravation of their mother's overall character, for she was stingy in all things: money, praise, the facts of her terrifying past.

And here was the other thing that made Dora's belated career choice surprising. After so many years of brushing away any mention of her past like some troublesome fly, Dora had chosen to make her own life the subject of her public speeches. She would tell complete strangers about the loss of every member of her family in the incinerators of Auschwitz, and about her inexplicable survival. The world, it seemed, would soon know more of Dora than either Mariana or Julian ever had.

"And this idea just occurred to you out of the blue?" Mariana asked in dismay. She, Julian, and their mother were eating their monthly lunch at a deli on Fairfax.

"A woman, she comes to our Ladies' Committee at the temple," Dora explained. "She said she needs speakers for the schools and museums. She tells us people are beginning to forget. I said, 'Lady, you came to the right place. These women without husbands, all they do is talk, talk, talk.' " Her once-a-week beauty parlor shellac bobbed excitedly on top of her head.

"And you agreed to this?" Mariana asked, still unable to grasp the facts.

"Who am I to say no?" Dora gazed around the open dining room, where the few aging Jews of the neighborhood huddled in orange Naugahyde booths, while around them buzzed a relentlessly tattooed gaggle of young people. "Oh, my Gut!" she exclaimed. "People your age don't even know the Holocaust existed!"

Mariana followed her mother's gaze. People her age? But this was just another of Dora's persistent tics: the refusal to grasp that her children were smack in the middle of their unremarkable lives.

"People our age are middle-aged," Mariana said aloud, turning to Julian. "Scary, isn't it?"

Julian shrugged. His boyish face allowed him some measure of deceit, although the years of abuse were finally etching a worn patina around his eyes. Still, at thirty-eight, he was entertaining enough to be kept in the back pockets of his richer, more successful Hollywood friends. A skinny Falstaff, Mariana thought. He was a charming escort to ladies in need, an ineffectual pretty boy for men in similar circumstances. Occasionally, Mariana would spy her brother's face in the deep background of a celebrity photo-op. He'd be the "and friend" to a recognizable substar. Mariana had no real idea how Julian made ends meet, and she never asked, afraid that the truth would be much more troubling than anything she could imagine.

His appetite was good today, she observed, but occasionally his movements were exaggerated, as if he were receiving a misfired electronic jolt. He repeatedly raked his fingers through his head of lank blond hair. Wasted, Mariana thought, or desperately in need of a fix.

"The ignorance of young people is unbe-leeeevable, no?" Dora continued.

"Young people get to be ignorant," Julian said. He reached across the table to gather up a handful of bagel chips from Mariana's plate with his spidery fingers. "It's called progress."

"So you like my idea?" Dora asked brightly.

"If it's what you want to do," Julian said, "I support you a hundred percent."

"My Mariana thinks it's silly. I can tell that face."

"I don't think it's silly."

Dora frowned. "Why are you so mean to me?"

"Mother," Mariana sighed.

For as long as Mariana could remember, Dora had navigated her life as this guileless, childlike individual. Forget that she had survived the camps. Or that she managed to get herself to America, find a husband, move across the continent, and start a dressmaking business. Or that, when he died five years later, she managed to raise her children on her own. Instead, Dora preferred the illusion that her survival was simply a quirk of fate. She was as surprised by it as a child would be by the sight of a red kite adrift in the sky.

"At least Julian loves me," Dora complained petulantly.

"I'm your boy," he said, scratching at a nonexistent bite on his chin.

"It's good, then. Mommy has a good idea," Dora pronounced and began making a show of searching for her wallet inside her purse.

Familiar with the routine, Mariana reached for the crumpled bills inside her bag and placed them on the table. "My treat," she said.

Dora clapped her hands together. "See?" she exclaimed. "You love me after all."

After dropping Dora off at her apartment on the corner of Gardner and Third, Mariana and Julian lingered in her car. The floor was littered with the detritus of Mariana's five-year-old daughter, Willow's, life: discarded juice boxes, hard plastic bubblegum machine prizes, a splatter of stray barrettes. Mariana considered what an archaeologist, thousands of years hence, would make of this find. Would it be possible to surmise a reasonable life from all this useless stuff? She tapped a pipe cleaner spider which hung from her rearview mirror and watched it spin lazily around on its string.

"She's an artist," Julian said.

"Willow or Mommy?"

Julian chuckled. "The ignorance of young people is astonishing, no?" he said in a perfect imitation.

"You should be an actor," Mariana said.

"I always am." He scratched his bare ankle where tendons pressed against his translucent skin like the roots of a tree.

"She meant us, of course," she said. "How ignorant we are. As though she wanted us to intuit her past without being told."

"Can you imagine carrying around that stuff all your life? She's finally doing something healthy-minded."

"Thank you, Mr. Lifetime of Self-Destruction. You use those ankles when the rest of the veins in your body collapse?"

"You read too many bad novels. Anyway, we're not talking about me."

"We never do."

Julian smiled enigmatically as he opened the passenger door. Mariana felt alarmed, as though he were getting out in the middle of moving traffic.

"Where are you going?" she called after him. "I'll drop you somewhere." She knew so little of his life. Whenever he left her, she felt him evaporate.

"I'm fine from here," he said. "Big kiss to Willow." He shut

the door and started off down Third Street. Mariana watched as
he blended in with the darkly clad Hasidim milling around an
unmarked shul. She smiled at the notion of resourceful Julian
finding some kid with coke-bottle glasses to deal drugs with.
He was a cunning survivor and had been since childhood—
wheedling better lunches in the schoolyard, dressing himself in
the latest fashions neither he nor their mother could afford. He
claimed to get these prized goods through trades, an explanation that was acceptable to Dora. Back then, Mariana did not
understand how much of himself he had to offer.

She had a week's worth of work waiting for her in the
museum lab—a crateful of bone shards to be cleaned, coded,
and analyzed. The La Brea Tar Pits were like prisons from
which forgotten criminals periodically emerged. Year after
year, important finds were made in the black muck outside the
museum doors and it was her job to prepare them for further
study.

She parked her car and walked past the garbage-strewn
park outside the museum. In deference to show business,
someone had constructed a *tableau vivant* in the still-bubbling
tar. A mastodon and a calf watched onshore while another
giant beast struggled vainly in the black, sticky lake. Day after
day, Mariana passed children standing at wire fence. They
curled their tiny fingers around the metal, awed by the
entrapment.

The museum itself was a backwater, the exhibits old and
unchanging. Mariana walked through the darkened rooms,
feeling the pleasurable sense of suspension they induced,

trapped as they were in the dual anachronisms of history and unfashionable architecture. Her job was a low-paying and tedious recompense for the years spent struggling to finance her studies. But she had grown used to the work and to this place, which seemed not part of the world but rather like a vapor, hovering above it.

Mattias was in the lab when she entered, hunched over a fragment. He'd held a similar laboratory job in Austria and had come to California a year earlier, primarily to surf. He'd been adept at picking up the mannerisms of that world, and he greeted Mariana each day with an aggressively blank smile. She could not imagine the force of will it took to be so resolutely uncommitted to any judgment. Once her initial frustration with his fecklessness abated, though, he became weirdly attractive to her. Now they had been sleeping together for four months.

Staring at his strong back, Mariana had a momentary impulse to surprise him with a hug from behind. But their relationship did not include these intimacies. They could have sex once a week, followed by sitting naked in his humid apartment in Venice, smoking and listening to a clanging foreign import. But a frankly warm embrace? It would be awkward and embarrassing for them both. So she watched as he worked. His thonged feet were planted squarely on the ground, his hips, clad in fluorescent orange surfer jams, swayed from side to side.

"Got something?" she said finally.

He turned quickly. "I didn't hear you come in. Long lunch?"

"My mother," she sighed, putting her purse in a metal file cabinet. She started to search for her work gloves.

"Hey, you rode in on her wave."

"Oh, spare me," she said, though she couldn't help smiling at the incongruity of his harsh Austrian accent and his surfer patois.

"I think this is something good." He motioned her over to his workstation.

Mariana leaned into his microscope, inhaling the odor of his salty skin. What she saw through the lens made her forget about him, though. Embedded in a chunk of tar was a fossilized tooth: a piece of history no longer missing.

"Awesome," Mattias said.

"Umm," she agreed, for she couldn't think of a better word.

"Mommee!" Willow screamed, when Mariana walked into the after-school room at the end of the day. Willow, her hair a mop of tangled dirty-blond ringlets, ran over and jumped up into her mother's arms. It always took Mariana a moment to adjust to the noisy room. Each child was in continual flux: changing games, rules, articles of clothing, eager to get bigger, move forward, be shed of the boring present.

"Baby," Mariana said, kissing Willow's dirty cheek. "How was your day?"

"Fine," Willow answered with her patented nonresponse.

"What did you do? What did you learn?"

"Bubble art."

"Bubble what?"

"It's just, oh, something to do with bubbles and . . . oh,

never mind." Willow gave an exasperated sigh. "And we had P.E.," she said, brightening.

"Okay," Mariana relented. "Want to get a Slurpee?"

"Yes, I do!" Willow shrieked. Her reactions were always extreme, as though she were living in a slightly more wondrous universe than everyone around her. Mariana received teachers' reports that Willow was often "somewhere else" and that it was difficult to keep the girl "on point." One teacher noted after a frustrating math exercise that Willow seemed determined to resist the truth.

They stopped at the 7-Eleven around the corner from the school, bought cherry Slurpees, then sat in the car sucking loudly on them. Willow's tongue and chin soon turned a chemical shade of red. She concentrated deeply, as though memorizing every moment of her treat's dissolution. This intensity reminded Mariana of Willow's father. He'd been a research fellow at the university. They had been together a year when she became pregnant. He'd poured himself into the project with scientific zeal, devouring pregnancy manuals and birthing guides. He'd been admirable during the home birth too, following the midwife's directions as impeccably as any surgical nurse. But on the second day of Willow's life, Mariana had caught him sitting on the bed staring impassively down at the baby in the bassinet like she was a perplexing bone shard.

"You're not in it for the long haul, are you?" she'd asked, knowing it was true as she said it. The next week, he'd moved out of her apartment, and a month later, out of town. He hadn't contacted her or Willow since.

As the years passed, she occasionally missed him the way

you might miss the directions to a board game. Willow had turned out to be a complicated person with an unhinged imagination. Dinner dishes were flying saucers, saltshakers were control knobs that would direct her to planets where the peas were sad and clamoring orphans. She would lean out the open window of their apartment and talk to strangers passing under her, or with people who were not there at all.

"Small airplanes fly faster than big airplanes," Willow announced, staring thoughtfully into the soggy paper cone of her Slurpee.

"Well," Mariana replied carefully, anticipating Willow's passionate defense, "that's not actually true."

"It is true," Willow said, her voice rising several octaves. "Today, in school, we went in a small airplane and we raced a big airplane and we won."

"Okay," Mariana said, hoping to avoid an argument. Perhaps the answer to Willow's character lay in this missing person of a father. Or perhaps her personality was hers alone, as inscrutable as any other.

"And we saw a dinosaur."

Mariana fired up the car. They stopped once more to pick up their daily takeout and headed home.

It was already dark by the time they reached Mariana's apartment building. After parking in the underground garage, she and Willow walked up the cement inner stairwell to the second floor. The complex was cheaply built—you could hear conversations coming through walls and smell the odors of different dinners as you passed apartment doors. The rent was good, though, and the building was reasonably secure, assuming that everyone remembered to shut the self-locking front door.

But when Mariana pushed open her own door, she gasped and instinctively pushed Willow behind her. Inside, a body lay sprawled on the living room couch. Mariana reached into her bag for a can of pepper spray, flicked on the lights, and prepared to attack, when she realized that this creature, dead with sleep, was her brother.

"How did you get in?" she demanded. Her fear turned into rage and she pummeled his thin shoulder until he roused.

"Uncle Julian!" Willow exclaimed delightedly, crawling onto the couch and jumping up and down.

"Jesus, cut it out!" Julian mumbled groggily, his arms shielding his face.

"What are you doing here?" Mariana said. "You scared the shit out of me."

"You said a bad word!" Willow screeched gleefully.

"What are you doing here?" Mariana repeated, ignoring her daughter.

"You gave me a key, remember?"

"I did not."

"Stop hitting me, will you?" Julian pleaded.

Mariana realized she was still punching him. "Willow, get off the couch," she ordered.

"It's okay," Julian said. He reached up and pulled Willow down onto the fading orange velvet. She threw her arm across his narrow chest and lay her head in the valley between his shoulder and neck.

"When you went away for the weekend last year and I watered the plants," he said. "You gave me a key."

"You gave me that key back." She remembered making sure that he had: the last thing she wanted was for her house key to be floating around his world. She had to protect Willow.

"I made a copy," he said sheepishly. "For in case."

This was a phrase from their childhood. Dora had a habit of forgetting things, like the fact that they would need money for the bus or lunch, or, on occasion, that she had children at all. Mariana and Julian had compensated by storing any spare change they could find in Julian's rain boot and keeping a stack of candy bars inside Mariana's school locker. Mariana sometimes thought of her mother as a circuit that would occasionally overload. At these times, Dora's ability to grasp the details of her life would disappear. Mariana and Julian had spent one entire night huddled underneath the stairwell when Dora had failed to arrive home after work. They had been too embarrassed to knock on the neighbor's door.

Mariana sat heavily on the arm of the couch. Willow sat up, straddled her uncle, and put her hands on either side of his face.

"I needed the key," he said to Willow.

"He needed it," Willow repeated, looking at her mother.

"Go open up the bags and lay out dinner," Mariana ordered.

Irked, Willow nevertheless complied, running into the tiny kitchen off the living room. Soon Mariana heard silverware scratching against the aluminum table, and plates cracking together dangerously.

" 'Open up the bags,' Mari? Do you ever cook?" Julian said.

"Do you ever think about other people?" she answered in a half whisper. "Willow is five years old."

"I needed someplace to go."

"You can always come here. You don't have to break in." She looked down at his face. His eyes were dark and glassy.

"You're high."

"I'm not."

"Your pupils are pinny. That's a sign."

He stretched his lanky body out so that his feet extended past the edge of the couch. "I love you," he said, smiling at her. "Pupils pinny. Sign of drug involvement." He was imitating her precise scientist's patter.

"Shut up."

"I can't be out there, Mari," he said, gesturing at the window. "It's like a drug sweepstakes. The parties. People practically hand you the stuff."

"You're hanging out with the wrong crowd."

"It's the only crowd that'll have me."

They were quiet for a moment. Mariana could hear Willow singing to herself in the kitchen. Julian reached for Willow's Olympic figure-skating Barbie on the coffee table and began to straighten her miniature skirt.

"Where's Heinz?" he asked.

"Mattias."

"Same difference."

"We're not at the hanging-out stage. Just the fucking stage."

"Really?" Julian propped himself higher. "Mari having mindless sex. How exciting."

Mariana caught a glimpse of what others must like about him. He was completely captivated by anything she might have to say, as if her little skirmishes in the wrinkled sheets of an aging make-believe surfer had profound meaning.

"Mindless? As opposed to your intimate trysts in Griffith Park?"

"You romanticize my life." He held Barbie in the air, executing deft pirouettes with her lifeless form. "I haven't had sex in years."

"Truth?"

But Julian only grinned. Mariana hit him in the arm again, and Barbie flew out of his hands onto the floor.

"Death to Barbie," he said.

Julian slept on the couch. Mariana woke more than once during the night to the sound of him retching in the bathroom. He was still sleeping the next morning when she walked out of her room and she worked quietly as she made coffee in the kitchen.

At seven-thirty, Willow awoke and threw herself on top of the damp clump of sheets on the couch. Julian sat up slowly. He was white and ragged. Mariana could see him struggle to appear alive for the girl. Judging from the floor beside the couch, he hadn't made it to the bathroom at least once. Mariana cleaned the mess quickly and started on breakfast when the phone rang.

"I have a job," Dora announced on the other end of the line.

"What kind of a job?" Mariana watched Julian and Willow play on the couch. She tried to think up a believable story to explain Julian's state to her daughter.

"To make my speech. You don't listen to me, Mariana, when I talk?"

"Already?"

"A week from Thursday. And I have nothing to wear."

"Buy yourself something new. You deserve it."

Julian perked up. "Alert the presses. The queen of the thrift shop wishes to make a new purchase."

"You will take me now," Dora declared. "First thing before everybody gets there. You'll pick me up."

"Saturday's my day for Willow," Mariana said, although one glance at Julian and she knew the day would be spent getting him through it. They'd tell Willow he had the flu.

"I can't drive myself," Dora said. "Not on the Sabbath."

"You can shop but you can't drive?"

"Don't be smart," Dora said. "Pick me up. Tell Willow I have a kiss for her."

"*Tell her I hev a keez for hair,*" Mariana muttered as she hung up the phone.

"Who has keys? What keys?" Willow asked.

"Get dressed," Mariana instructed. "We're going shopping with Nana."

The discount store was teeming by the time Mariana, Dora, and Willow arrived. Ranks of women snaked their way between dress racks with warlike determination. Dora froze in place. Mariana pushed her mother in front of her with one hand, grabbed Willow with the other, and guided them across the crowded floor. Dora allowed herself to be pushed along by the press of people around her. When they reached a logjam of shoppers, Mariana reeled Dora back for a change of direction. She caught her mother's gaze: the old woman's eyes were blank, as if Dora had chosen to disappear.

But when they arrived at Ladies' Dresses, Dora snapped into action, rifling through the racks with ferretlike intensity. Her seamstress's eye studied linings, finishing stitches, and button-holes; she dismissed most garments with withering lip sput-ters. When another woman ventured too close, Dora shot her a look and the woman backed off.

Meanwhile, Willow made for the racks of chained furs. She lost herself in them until all Mariana could see were the girl's red sandals and bony ankles. Willow's disembodied voice exclaimed "Sale of the century!" and "It's a steal!" but Mariana could not make out much else.

Finally, Dora selected two dresses, one purple, the other blue.

"Purple! Purple!" Willow cried, emerging from the furs and wrapping herself in the shimmery synthetic fabric of Dora's choices. "Purple is the color of kings! You will be the king and I will be the lady-in-waiting and I will lift your robes as you walk."

"What is she talking about?" Dora asked.

"Let's try the dresses on," Mariana suggested, wanting the trip to be over as soon as possible.

In the communal changing room, women faced scuffed walls while they pulled on garments. Others jockeyed for position in front of the room's single floor-length mirror.

"Everyone's naked!" Willow shouted.

Dora set her purse on a folding metal chair and hung her dresses up on a free hook. "Everyone is like animals in here. Cows!" she muttered, positioning Mariana and Willow directly behind her so they formed a human curtain. Willow took to the task, spreading her arms out and rocking her body from side to side.

Dora pulled her sweater over her head. When she pushed down her elastic-waisted pants, Mariana noticed how solid her buttocks and hips still were. Mariana imagined how she would look, grown into this body in another thirty years. Minus, of course, the tattoo etched on her mother's arm. When Mariana was small, she had asked about the numbers. "Oh, that!" Dora had sighed, as though bored by their tenacious presence after all those years. "I put these numbers on my arm to cheat on a math test." Mariana had asked to know what the word *cheat* meant and Dora had told her it meant to trick God. Then she narrowed her gaze accusatorily, ending any further discussion.

When Mariana had grown older and heard the truth from others, she tried to engage her mother in the kitchen one afternoon. But Dora did not respond, as though she could not hear the words through the shield of steam rising from the pot of wilting cabbage. And later still, when Mariana had asked outright what happened to her mother during the war, Dora's expression became empty and Mariana felt her mother slip away. In her place stood a phantom mother, sewing the same garment, fussing with an identical strand of loose hair. Her own mother had gone temporarily missing. Mariana had been so frightened that she never asked her questions again.

The bust line of the purple dress cut awkwardly across Dora's broad chest.

"Whoever made this dress needs to go back to school," she said, taking the garment down off her shoulders and studying the inside seams. "Who has a bosom under her neck?"

Willow exploded into giggles. Dora tried on the blue dress. She was more forgiving of the simple shirtwaist that grabbed her gently around her thick middle. She reached for the price tag dangling underneath one armpit.

"One hundred twenty-five dollars!" she exclaimed.

"It's been a long time since you've been in the stores," Mariana said.

"I could make this dress for half the price! A third, even." Dora pulled the dress over her head and held it out in front of her as though it now had an offensive odor. She folded back the neckline. "My Gut!" she said. "It's not even double-faced!"

"I'll buy it for you," Mariana offered.

"You will do no such thing."

"You should have something new to wear," Mariana said, recognizing the rhythms of the old routine.

"I'll find something in my closet. I'll get out my machine."

"Mother, you're speaking in front of strangers. You can't wear a dress from thirty years ago."

"They're only students," Dora mused. "Still, I don't want to be disrespectful."

"Of course you don't."

Dora sighed deeply. She handed the garment to her daughter and looked away. "Cut the price off, my Mariana. I can't think of the crime of it another second."

Mariana took Willow's hand and stood by the door to the dressing room as her mother shimmied back into her own clothes. All around, women worked and worried, patted their ample stomachs, sucked in their cheeks, and tilted their chins to the mirror, making themselves into images from some real or imagined youth. Mariana wondered what girl her mother saw when she looked into that glass.

Julian stayed at Mariana's apartment for the next week. His withdrawal left him irritable and frequently overcome by chills and nausea. He complained that his blood ached. One night, Mariana returned home to find him in the steaming bathtub, fully clothed. "I can't get warm," he mumbled through his shivers. She watched sadly, as the dye from his blue jeans seeped into the water. An hour later, she found him stripping off his nightclothes and throwing open windows. He said his ears were sweating.

Mariana nursed him with hot-water bottles, ice packs, blankets, and food. By week's end, his chills subsided and his color returned. The following Monday, when Mariana and Willow came back from their day, they found the house cleaned and organized, and dinner already prepared.

"Where are the takeout bags?" Willow asked suspiciously.

"Bags indeed!" Julian bellowed.

"You went out?" Mariana asked carefully, studying her brother for signs that this sudden optimism was drug-induced. "How was the real world?"

"I walked straight to the market and straight back. I kept my head down the whole time. It was brutal."

"You should watch where you're going, Uncle Julian," Willow said. "You might trip."

"Exactly," Julian said, running his hands through Willow's hair. He rolled his eyes at Mariana and she let out her breath, relieved. He was clean.

That night, Mariana slept restlessly. Her mother's speech was three days away. Mariana could imagine scenarios of disaster: Dora would get up on the stage and freeze. Or she would speak so unintelligibly that people would have no idea what she was saying. Or she would forget that she'd made the plan in the first place and not show up at all.

The next day, she took a break from work and dialed her mother. "Do you think you're ready?" she asked.

"Ready? It's today? Oh, my God!"

"It's not today, Mother. But you need to be prepared."

"I have blue shoes. But I need a bag. You'll find me a good bag?"

"I was thinking maybe you want to go over your speech."

"What is this 'go over'?"

The door of the lab opened and Mattias came in. A thin layer of sand clung to his calves.

"Practice," Mariana continued. "Rehearse what you want to say."

"I know what happened to me. I have to practice this?"

Mariana's stomach tightened. She had heard and read countless stories of brutal torture and miraculous escape. She'd seen movies, some painfully raw, others more comfortably cushioned by movie stars and excellent lighting. The stories were all awful, but they floated in a numbing stew of unbearable things that happen to other people. Dora's tragedy would be particular and close.

"Talking in front of people," Mariana said weakly, "is harder than you think."

"Acch!" Dora scoffed. "Get me a blue purse."

When Mariana finally hung up the phone, Mattias was putting his lab coat over his T-shirt and shorts.

"She's going to make it up as she goes along," Mariana said helplessly.

"Improvisation is cool."

"It's going to be a disaster."

"Fitting to the subject, no?"

She watched as he found the materials he needed for the day's work.

"I suppose these are things you must talk about in your country," she mused. "What happened during the war?"

"Umm," he said vaguely.

"You must learn about it in school. The way we learn about slavery. Or the Japanese camps."

"Sure, sure. But when I was a child, you know, we studied up until 1935 and then started again in 1950." He held his hands in the air as though to frame the gap.

"Really?" She was stunned.

"More or less," he said simply. "You do not teach children to be ashamed."

"Children need to know the truth," she said. "Otherwise, something is always missing."

"We knew," he said. "Not knowing something is a kind of knowing."

"No," she said resolutely. "That's just surfer bullshit."

Mattias smiled. "Okay," he said without rancor.

Her face was hot and her throat tight. She had to leave the lab to keep from screaming.

That night, Mariana put Willow to bed and, although ambivalent, prepared for her weekly rendezvous with Mattias. Ten minutes before she was scheduled to leave, Esperanza, her usual sitter, called to say that her son's baby-sitter was ill and she would not be able to come stay with Willow.

"She pays someone to watch her kid so she can come and watch your kid?" Julian asked as Mariana hung up the phone.

Mariana nodded, pulling her beeper out of her pocket and laying it on the table. "I pay more than she pays, so she comes out on top. I have to call Mattias."

"I'm here," Julian said. "And I don't charge anything."

"You want to baby-sit?"

"Willow's asleep. How hard could it be? If she wakes up and asks for a glass of water, I'll get her a glass of water."

Mariana looked down uncomfortably. She knew that if she said no, her distrust of Julian would hang between them. Still, they were talking about Willow. Mariana practically required police records before she let people baby-sit her daughter.

"I don't know," she said. "I'm tired, anyway."

Julian lay a hand on hers. "Let me do it, Mari," he said. "I can do it." He winced like a stray dog who's accustomed to being hit.

"I know you can," she consented, reaching for her beeper. "Okay."

She and Mattias had sex in his apartment. The ocean air was chilly and damp. This, combined with their conversation that day, made Mariana edgy. She had placed her beeper on the floor next to his futon, and occasionally, as they rolled around, she would make sure to look for it. Afterwards, Mattias sat naked and cross-legged, staring up at her while she dressed.

"You weren't really there, were you?" he asked.

"Where?"

He cocked his head towards the futon.

"No," she admitted, buttoning her blouse. "Was it necessary?"

"I suppose not."

She tucked her shirt into her jeans. "Sorry."

"Don't apologize. It's sad, though, not to be where you are."

She looked down at his muscular, aging body. "You were someone totally different before you came to Los Angeles, weren't you?"

"In some ways."

"It's that easy for you to forget yourself?"

"No one's stopping me."

He stretched his naked body across the bed. She could imagine his skeleton inside his narrow body, the hip socket, femur, and patella neatly fitting into one another. Lodged in those bones was his inescapable history.

"Hand me my beeper."

He held the beeper in his hands. "Drug deals?" he teased.

A hot flush raced through her body. Wouldn't Julian have beeped her if there'd been a problem? "I have to go home right now," she said urgently. "Give it to me."

He handed her the beeper, then lifted up his hands in surrender as she left.

Julian was sitting on the couch, staring at the door when she returned. His eyes were bleary with exhaustion. "I was afraid to sleep in case I wouldn't hear Willow," he explained.

Her relief made her weak. She fell next to him on the couch. "You're allowed to sleep," she said, brushing hair from his eyes. "Even Esperanza sleeps."

"I was so worried the whole time. I didn't want to fuck up."

"You didn't. You did a great job."

He sighed and shook his head. "God, that was hard."

They sat quietly together.

"Mommy called," he said finally. Reaching into his pocket, he retrieved a crumpled piece of paper and handed it to Mariana. She read an address for a girl's high school in Brentwood where the talk was to be given.

"We're supposed to take her," he said. "She wants to be there early."

"It will be like going to watch a car wreck on purpose," Mariana said. She waited for him to agree, but he tilted his head back against the couch and shut his eyes. She felt his removal like an ache; in a moment, he was sleeping.

Dora wanted to be at the school two hours before her talk was scheduled. Unable to justify the cost of Esperanza for the extra time, Mariana left Julian to entertain Willow and drove Dora to the school. Later, she would return home, get Willow settled with Esperanza, and drive back to the school with Julian in time for the speech.

Dora was waiting outside her apartment when Mariana drove up, looking like a neat package in her dress and matching shoes.

"Where's my blue bag?" Dora asked, peering into the back seat of the car.

"I forgot," Mariana said.

"Acch," Dora said, and got into the passenger seat.

As they drove west, Dora chatted about trivial things: her challah bread was nearly stale when she brought it home from the store, her neighbor was making a mess with the garbage cans. "And me, an old lady, I'm stooping down to clean up orange rinds and what else!"

"Why are you doing this, Mother?" Mariana asked finally.

"What is 'this,' my Mariana?"

"Talking. Today. Why now, after all this time?"

Dora made a dismissive sputter and looked out the side window.

Mariana dropped Dora at the school and returned home. Willow sat alone in the middle of the living room, constructing a pillow fort and populating it with stuffed animals. Mariana stalked through the apartment looking for her brother. When she could not find him, her heart began to race.

"Where's Julian?" she demanded of her daughter.

"He had to run an errand. He'll come back."

"How long ago did he leave?"

Willow fixed her mother with a withering look. "I can't tell time yet."

"Oh, my God!" Mariana cried out. Her mind inhabited the terrible scenarios of what might have happened to her child, alone in the apartment. She crouched down, clutching her daughter by the shoulders. "Are you okay? Did he do anything to you?"

Willow spoke slowly, as though explaining something to a toddler: "He made me a snack in the kitchen. I haven't eaten it yet because we're busy here." She gestured to the orchestration of dolls. "Miss Bear said 'shit' and we're going to behead her."

"Oh, my God," Mariana repeated, standing up slowly. She felt she was two people: one stood here, maintaining her composure for the sake of her daughter, while the other stormed around the house, ripping plates off of shelves and cracking them against walls. Her brother was a drug addict. She had trusted a drug addict to take care of her child.

The doorbell rang. She raced to it, ready to greet Julian with her fury. But it was Esperanza who smiled up at her. She had a Mayan face as wide and gentle as a lake. Her smile fell as she tried to comprehend Mariana's expression.

"Mariana? Am I late?"

But before Mariana could speak, Willow bounced into the room and rushed into Esperanza's arms. "Esperanza, my love!" she squealed, as she dragged her baby-sitter into her bedroom.

Mariana checked her watch. Her mother would be speaking in an hour and it would take her nearly that time to drive across town. She walked into Willow's room and beckoned Esperanza into the hallway. "Don't let anybody in, okay?" she said in a low voice.

"Sure," Esperanza replied. "Same as always. We'll keep the door locked and I have your beeper number."

"I mean anybody," Mariana insisted. "Even if Willow knows them. Even if it's my brother. Okay? I don't want you to let my brother in. Don't let Willow twist your arm, either." When Esperanza looked worried, Mariana tried to lighten her tone. "It's just that he's not well," she said. "I don't want to expose you guys to the flu or anything."

"Okay," Esperanza said uncertainly.

Mariana kissed Willow and left the house, making sure to shut the self-locking door on her way out. She checked her key chain; Julian's extra key was hanging there along with all her others.

She drove out of her underground garage and headed past the grand houses fronting the boulevard. The sidewalks that had once bustled with people promenading past the homes of bankers and movie stars were lifeless now but for the incessant rush of freeway-bound cars. She saw only one fellow in the near distance, sitting on a bus bench. His head was in his hands, his fingers splayed over his skull like a cap. Even without seeing the man's face, she recognized the agony etched in his posture. A homeless man, she thought. One of those tragic souls whose mental illness drags him around the city like a confused tour guide. But when she drove nearer, she realized the man was her brother.

Pulling over to the curb, she stopped her car and got out in front of Julian. He did not look up or even move and she wondered if he was dead. "Julian! Julian!" she cried out, kneeling and shaking his shoulder.

Finally, his body shifted. "Mari," he said groggily. "I'm sorry, Mari. I'm sorry."

"You left Willow alone," she said, her rage returning. "What if something had happened?"

"I'm going to go back," he whispered. "I promise."

"She's five years old. What if there had been a fire?"

He said nothing and she stood up, moving a few steps away from him as he cowered on the bench.

"It's my fault," she said. "I don't know what I was thinking, leaving her with you." She walked a tight circle in place as she berated herself. Finally, she stopped and refocused her anger on him. "What are you doing here?" she demanded.

He looked up at her with his drugged, half-lidded eyes. She had her answer.

"Oh, Julian," she said sadly.

"I couldn't do it," he said. "Everything was so bright and loud."

"What was?"

"The world. The way things are. It hurts."

They were silent for a moment.

"Mommy," he wailed.

Mariana looked at her watch. She had less than an hour to get across town. She crouched down and put her hand over his delicate one. "I'm going to go hear her talk," she said. "Are you coming?"

He looked down between his knees.

"Julian, you can't go back to my house. Not like this."

"I know," he said. "Go."

"I won't leave you here."

"Mari, go," he said firmly. "Please leave me alone."

The school, an elaborate Spanish building, stood regally over-looking Sunset Boulevard. Mariana parked and quickly walked through the carved wooden doors of the main entrance. The auditorium doors were closed and a few people turned their heads when she slipped inside. Dora was standing at the podium, her body nearly dwarfed by the baroque lectern. Mariana found an empty chair and sat down next to a young girl.

Mariana could not focus on her mother. Her mind was like a frantic bird darting here and there around the room. The girls were pressed up against one another in the closely set folding chairs. Mariana was overcome by the variety of hair—blond, brown, straight, curly, braided, and cornrowed. Some girls sat or slouched, hands dangling between knobby or fleshy knees. Others clutched the sides of the metal seats, or haphazardly held hands with a friend. Some faces were doughy with adolescence, others, were smooth and clear, as though having recently been shed of another skin. The girls' newness took Mariana aback. She was reminded of herself long ago as she waited for her mother to tell her things.

"I have no story to tell you," Dora began haltingly.

Mariana moved to the edge of her seat, ready to stand and save her mother from embarrassment.

"I made no kind of exciting escape that you can read about in books," Dora continued, her gnarled brogue gathering strength. "I survived because I wasn't killed. It's simple, really, but as old as I am, I cannot understand it."

She stopped and looked down at the lectern for an uncomfortably long pause. Mariana could hear the girls move in their squeaky seats. Heads tilted as a ripple of whispers moved across the auditorium. Dora lifted her chin and stared out into the audience. Her expression was empty. Mariana could hear her own young voice. *Mommy, it's late and we've had no dinner. Mommy, do you hear me? Mommy, where are you now?*

Finally, Dora continued. "There are words I have not spoken," she said. "Because I was afraid that when I said these words, I would start to scream. But now I think I have been screaming all my life. So, today I will speak and maybe I will find my quiet."

The girls sat still. Mariana's body ached with what felt like forty years of waiting. Dora began again.

"I can tell you that my mother had a beautiful smell." She focused on the girls now. They listened, lips parted gently as if to take the words into their mouths. Dora continued more boldly. "When I came home from school, I could smell when she was in the house. And when she was not, I could open up one of her drawers and smell her there in her fine soft under-clothes. I remember her smell on the train too, even when I was crowded in so tight I could not see her face. . . . This smell is lost to me now. But not the sound of the train. *Pock-e-ta, pock-e-ta, pock-e-ta. . . .*"

Mariana slid back into her seat. The words tumbled over her like shattering glass.

THE PASSENGER

I have a ring in my nose and a ring in my navel, and people make assumptions about me. None of them are true. I'm not a punk or a slave, a biker chick or a fashion hag.

I drive a limo. I take people where they want to go—to parties and airports, to score drugs at a ranch house or a piece of ass at a hotel bar. On any given night, I'll be taking the curves on Mulholland, hitting a prom in Northridge, or, if I'm lucky, flying the straight shot out the highway to Malibu. People think Los Angeles is the same everywhere—all palm trees and swimming pools. But some nights you need a passport and a two-way dictionary just to get from Hancock Park to Koreatown.

Ruthanne's my dispatcher. I've never met her but she's

probably the person I talk to most. Once I saw her red jacket hanging off a chair at the office. It had a dog appliquéd across the back. Normally someone who would wear that jacket would have nothing to say to me, and so, in a sense, not meeting has brought us closer. Right now, her voice crackles over my car radio.

"EX-LAX," she says, using her helium balloon voice. "Who wants to shit or get off the pot?"

EX-LAX is her shorthand for saying there's a pickup at LAX, the airport. She says "re-lax" when you have to make your second airport trip. Ha, ha, ha, right? But I'm smiling.

I pick up my handset. "Twenty-two. I'm all over it." We're required to use our call number, but Ruthie never does. She calls me by my name, Babe.

"Okay, Babe," she says. "You're picking up two Chins outside international baggage."

"No way."

"Yes way," she says. "You'll have to circle the drain."

I click off. The usual airport routine is that I park the limo and wait at the arrivals gate, holding a piece of cardboard with a stranger's name on it. Finally, a passenger comes off the plane. He'll smile when he sees his name, delighted that he's the same guy he was before he took off. Sometimes he'll be so relieved that he'll shake my hand, like I care one way or another. It's moments like these that kill me.

But meeting someone outside baggage is an ordeal. Security is tight, and you can't wait by the curb for more than twenty seconds before some uniform appears, telling you to scram. So you have to drive around and around until you actually see the pickup.

I click on my radio again. "It could take an hour," I complain.

"You vant I should give it to someone else, *daah-link*?" Ruthie answers, doing her Gabor sisters impersonation.

"No," I say quickly. International is promising in other ways—people are often confused by the exchange rate. I once got a hundred-dollar tip from an Indian family that had fastened their suitcases together with electrical tape. I felt bad about taking it, but not so bad about having it.

I'm twenty-three. I live alone in a second-story box on Lincoln Boulevard. I had a boyfriend for a while. I liked him, then I didn't. I have a few friends left over from high school, and we go drinking sometimes, but lately I'm not sure why. We get together and moan about rent, or we get worked up telling stories we've told before. We end up staring into our drinks because facing each other is like looking into a mirror in bad lighting.

A few years ago, my mother left L.A. to join a spiritual community in the desert. This makes it sound like she's living in a collection of gassy, glowing matter; in fact, it's a bunch of trailers on a scrubby piece of land near a Marine base.

After she left, I worked as a waitress, a copy-shop clerk, a messenger—all those jobs you get when you have nothing but a couple of community college credits in highly useless things like world literature. The difference between me and the other

employees was that I didn't want to be something else. With all
the other people it was, "I work in a copy shop, but I really
want to act." Or, "I sell subscriptions over the phone, but I
have this great idea for an Internet company." Not that I want
to drive a car for the rest of my life, but I'm willing to say that
driving is what I do for now.

The fifth time I circle international baggage, people begin
to pour out the doors. Most of the passengers wear wrinkled
nylon track suits and baseball caps with American logos—
walking advertisements for a place they're seeing for the first
time. These people look dazed. All but a few are Asian and I
have no idea how I'm going to find my fare. Then I see a man
and a woman standing at the curb with a very large black suitcase between them, and for some reason I know that they are
my Chins. She's wearing a neatly cut jacket and a matching
skirt. Her black high heels are so polished they reflect the
lights overhead. He wears a double-breasted suit that hangs
loosely over his thin body. His hair is swooped back into a
gentle pompadour, and it's shiny with whatever goop he put
into it. You'd never guess that these two had just spent the day
on an airplane.

"Mr. and Mrs. Chin?" I call out of the passenger-side window.

They don't respond for a moment, but then they nod
enthusiastically. I pop the trunk and hop out of the car. I reach
for their suitcase, but Mr. Chin waves me away and points
towards the back seat.

"It's safer to put it in the trunk," I explain. "If the car stops
suddenly, the case could fly into your face."

They both smile, as if I've said something amusing but not exactly funny, and I realize that they don't understand a word I'm saying. I go for the suitcase again, but Mr. Chin steps in front of me, shaking his head. Mrs. Chin slides into the back seat like a swan, her legs pressed together, and holds out her hands to take the suitcase, which Mr. Chin pushes inside. Finally, he tucks himself neatly into the space left over and waits for me to shut the door. I think for a minute about pressing the point: it's company policy to put luggage in the trunk. If the Chins got hit with that hard plastic bag, they could sue and I'd be out of a job in the blink of an eye. But I let it go. People do things a million different ways. It's when you interfere that guns are drawn.

I get into the driver's seat, and Mr. Chin hands me a piece of paper through the privacy window. They want to go to Tarzana. I'm surprised. I would have thought they were visiting relatives in Monterey Park or staying in one of the downtown hotels. I call my destination in to Ruthanne.

"Tarzana," she repeats after me, and she gives her trademark jungle yodel.

I start the car and head towards the 405. It's still early and I have eight hours of road ahead.

The first time my mother tried to off herself, I was nineteen, already living alone, working shifts at an industrial laundry on Highland. So she called me to tell me.

"Babe," she said. "I'm leaving now."

"You're calling me to tell me you're leaving the house?"

"I'm leaving," she said. "In the final sense of the word."

"Delia," I said, the way I did when I wanted to get her attention, "what the hell are you talking about?"

She said she had taken an entire bottle of Xanax. She was getting yawny and slurry as we were talking, and I couldn't get her to tell me how many pills had been in the bottle. But, since she usually avoided taking her pills when she needed them, I figured that "entire" might be the truth.

"Don't move," I said. "Don't do anything."

When I got to her shabby rental in Laurel Canyon, she was sitting on her couch with her legs crossed underneath her. Her orange dress, missing half its sequined flowers, covered her knees like a tent. Bubbles of spit shone on her chin and there was vomit on her dress.

"Babe!" she said, as if I were dropping in for a surprise visit.

"How many did you take?" I asked. The bottle of pills was on the coffee table.

"Just a couple," she said. "I started to gag and then everything just came up and out." She giggled and covered her mouth like a girl on a date. "Want some tea? Or I could make us some lunch?"

"I have to go back to work," I said. "They'll dock my pay."

"Okay," she said, pouting. She played with the sequins on her dress. "I'm fine, I guess."

"I'll come back later," I said. "I'll bring you dinner."

"That would be nice." Her voice was drifting away, like some balloon a kid had let go of. She closed her eyes. "How's the laundry, Babe?"

"How?"

"Yeah. What's it like?"

"It's like dirty sheets getting clean."

"Um," she said. She smiled and nodded as though she were remembering some favorite childhood dessert. Her long hair had begun to make her look older and I could see age spots on her chest.

I went to work, where I unloaded soggy restaurant table-cloths and hospital sheets from the washing machines and crammed them into carriers strung from the ceiling. After eight hours, my apron was soaked and my hands were water-logged, and I was a little high off the dryer fumes. When I walked out onto Highland, I had the feeling I was swimming. The noise of the traffic was like the rubbery sounds you hear underwater.

Later that night, I brought bad Mexican takeout up to my mother. She was asleep in her bed. Her forehead was sweaty and cool. I watched her breathe a few times, then turned on the TV so she would have company when she woke up. I put the food in the refrigerator with a note to remind her to take the burrito out of the Styrofoam container before she reheated it.

Mr. Chin has something stuck in his teeth. He's working at it, first with his forefinger, then with the nail of his pinkie. Finally, he gives up, runs his tongue across his teeth, stares out the window. The traffic is starting to get a little thick for my taste, and the radio crackles on: Ruthanne, announcing a pickup in Sherman Oaks at eight-thirty.

I reach for my handset. "Twenty-two. I'll take it."

"Goody," she says. "Recording studio. Could be a *gen-u-ine* rock star."

"Goody," I shoot back. "I'll make sure he doesn't pee in the ashtray."

I cut across two lanes and exit the freeway at Sunset. I hop onto Sepulveda to save ten minutes, so I can get to the fare in time. The Chins don't register the route change, so I don't explain it. Sepulveda dips and bends underneath the freeway's underpasses, and as we swing around the curves, the Chins sway back and forth in perfect unison. *Weebles wobble but they don't fall down!* I remember this from TV somewhere when I was a kid. St. Louis? Cleveland? Driving sometimes puts me in this dreamy place where I remember strange details from my life: in one city, a bedspread covered with pictures of Cinderella; in another, the way you had to move the kitchen table to open the refrigerator. Miles go by like this without my noticing them; sometimes I'll reach a destination and have no idea how I got there.

Orange lights are flashing somewhere in my consciousness. My attention snaps back to the road. Up ahead, I see emergency vehicles and warning lights. We slow down and soon we aren't moving at all.

Mr. Chin bends forward to look out the windshield.

"Traffic," I explain. "Probably an accident."

He leans back and says something in Chinese to his wife. From her handbag, she takes out a mirror and a lipstick, which she applies with two perfect swipes. She purses her lips together, judges the result disinterestedly.

Ten minutes later, we are sitting in the same place, boxed in on one side by a line of cars; on the other, the road gives way to a gully. News choppers hover overhead. I pick up my radio.

"This is Twenty-two. Come in, Dispatch."

"I'm coming, I'm coming, I'm—unh!" Ruthie groans.

"You're a freak, you know that?" I say.

"This is what you're hogging the frequency to tell me?"

"It's molasses out here. Better take me off the Sherman Oaks."

"Not to worry. I think it was Captain and Tenille."

"Who?"

"You're making me feel old, Babe."

"I'm gonna need a lot of quickies later to make up on my tips," I say.

"I'll take care of you," she says. "Just sit tight."

"That's all I can do."

I sign off and watch the traffic flowing easily on the south-bound side of Sepulveda. You can be stuck or you can be going places. Usually it's just a matter of luck.

When I was eleven, my mother and I lived in Cleveland. All winter, the city was the color of dirty dishwater. People wore heavy coats and boots over their shoes and worried their way across icy streets, as though the roads were covered with nails. We'd come up from Pensacola and had nothing warmer to wear than sweatshirts, so my mother took us to the Salvation Army, where I picked out a hot-pink snow jacket and some blue boots that were a size too big. When I walked, my heels rubbed up and down inside, and after a few weeks, all my socks had matching holes.

We lived in a part of town where every house was cut up into four equal apartments, like a kid's baloney sandwich. We had the bottom left-hand quarter. At school, a girl told me I lived in the "bad" part of town. What she really meant was that it was the "black" part of town, and it was true: we were the only white people on our block. But we had just come from shitty neighborhoods in the South, and we knew how to get along.

The only nice thing for blocks around was a temple. It had a big gold dome and walls of polished stone, and had been built when this was still the good part of town. Now it was stuck here with no place to go, like the fat girl at the dance. After school, I often took the bus to the temple, where my mother worked as a cleaning lady. She'd make me sit quietly in the pews as she dusted the altar. The pews were covered with a rough maroon material and scratched the backs of my legs when I wore a skirt. I'd pass the time staring up at the dome, wondering whether all that gold was real or fake and whether I could climb up and scrape it off with my fingernails.

My mother hated Cleveland. She said that it was an ugly city, that the lake was so polluted it had caught on fire once, that months without sun made the people depressed and crazy. I wondered why she'd picked Cleveland if she felt this way, but I never asked. I knew that certain questions made her nervous.

One day, after my mother was finished up at the temple, we took a bus to a part of town I'd never seen. All the buildings were one-story brick, with matching green roofs. There were no stores, there were "shoppes." Everything was very clean. We stopped in a coffee shop and sat at a booth. Usually, when we ate out, I understood that I was to order the cheapest thing on the menu or share whatever my mother had. But this time she said, "You want the steak plate? Have the steak plate. That's what I'm having."

I ordered the steak plate. We didn't talk much, and about twenty minutes later a man came in with a girl a few years older than me. The coffee shop wasn't crowded, but when he got to our booth he stopped and asked if they could sit with us. My mother said yes, if they wanted. The man sat down. The girl looked upset, but he told her to sit, and she did.

The waitress came with our plates, and the man ordered a BLT for him and a grilled cheese for the girl. I felt embarrassed about my steak and I stopped eating.

"Eat your food," my mother ordered, so I did.

The man had a wide face with two strong lines that cut down each cheek like the biggest dimples I'd ever seen. He didn't take off his coat and hat, and he drank his glass of ice water with his gloves on. He caught me looking at him and he smiled. My mother didn't talk to him and he didn't talk to her. We just ate, and when the waitress brought their food the man and the girl ate too. The girl had long hair and it kept getting in her way. At one point, she found a hair in the melted cheese of her sandwich and started to pull. She pulled and pulled for what seemed a long time, concentrating as though she were playing a game with herself.

"It's mine," she determined when it finally came out, and continued to eat.

"You have long hair," my mother said. "You have to take care of that hair."

This seemed to stop everything. The man stopped chewing

and put his sandwich down. The girl looked at him as if she weren't sure what she was supposed to do.

"Answer the lady," he said.

"I brush it a hundred strokes in the morning and at night."

"Somebody must have taught you that," my mother said. I wasn't sure whether she was asking or telling. The girl didn't say anything.

We finished our steaks, and my mother washed hers down with coffee, then reached behind her and inched herself back into her coat. She slid out of the booth and turned to me.

"All right, Babe," she said. "We're done."

I was confused. We hadn't asked for a check and we hadn't left any money. But I put on my pink parka and followed my mother out the door and onto the street.

"I think we forgot to pay," I said once we were headed into the freezing wind towards the bus stop.

"We paid, all right," she said.

Another twenty minutes, and the traffic on Sepulveda hasn't moved a foot. I turn to talk to the Chins.

"Don't worry about the time. It's a flat rate."

They both smile, having no idea what I just said.

Ten minutes later, the Chins start to argue. He thinks one thing, she thinks another. That's all I can make out. She gestures once or twice towards the suitcase. Their voices yo-yo up and down like a twelve-year-old boy's.

I see a cop about fifty feet in front of us. He's moving down the line of cars.

"Look!" I say. "Policeman here! He tell us!" I'm talking like a racist pig, but it seems like they might understand me if I skip some words.

Mr. Chin makes a low, deep rumble in his throat. I open my window and call out to the cop. He comes up to the car.

"What's up?" I ask.

"Accident," he says. He has a narrow face and a nose that bends to the right.

"Just when I decide to take the fast route, right?"

"Happened over two hours ago."

"Oh," I say, realizing it doesn't take two hours to clean up a fender bender. "Somebody die?"

The cop nods. "Kids." There's a sad disgust in his voice. "My daughter wants one of those," he says, looking at my nose ring. "I told her it looks like you have a piece of dirt on your nose, or worse. No offense or anything."

"She's not doing it for you," I say. "No offense or anything."

For a second, he looks like he's going to get mad, but then he smiles.

"Ain't that the truth," he says.

He looks back at the Chins, who have gotten very quiet. I don't blame them. They've probably heard about the L.A.P.D. That Rodney King video was shown something like five hundred times a day all over the world.

The cop nods towards the Chins. "Airport?"

"Don't speak a word of English either."

"Welcome to L.A.," he says. I can't tell if he's talking about the Chins or to them. Then I hear a sound, like a muffled moan, coming from the back seat. I look in the rearview. Is Mrs. Chin getting sick in my car?

"Are you all right back there?" I say.

Mr. Chin looks up. His face has come alive, as though someone flipped a switch.

"Okay," he says. "Everything okay here."

"You speak English?" I say, amazed and a little pissed.

The cop leans into the car to get a closer look at the Chins.

"There's been a bad accident," he says. "Car crash." He mimes driving, then slaps his hands together, looking pleased with his little bit of community service.

"Yes, absolutely," Mr. Chin says. He nods his head, trying to look like he understands what's going on. Suddenly I feel a little sorry for him.

"Well, that's all she wrote," the cop says, slapping his palms down on my door. "You'll see it all on the ten o'clock news." He motions with his chin towards the sky where the choppers circle, their tails dangling above their bodies like wasps.

Just as he leaves, I hear the sound again. It's coming from the suitcase. The Chins start arguing loudly.

"Jesus," I say to nobody in particular. "What the hell is going on back there?"

Mrs. Chin cries out as if she'd been stabbed, and Mr. Chin screams at her. The car in front of me inches forward, the first movement in about an hour. In the rearview, I see the cop turn around and start to jog back to the scene of the accident.

"Here we go," I say as I put my foot on the gas. But just then Mr. Chin opens his door.

"Shut the car door," I yell. "We're moving!"

But Mr. Chin is already out on the side of the road, gesturing back at Mrs. Chin to hand him the suitcase. Before she has a chance to, he reaches in and yanks it from the car. Mrs. Chin follows, her skirt sliding up her thighs. The car in front of me has moved at least twenty feet and the ones behind me are honking.

"Are you crazy?" I scream at the Chins. "Get back in the fucking car!"

By now, every car on Sepulveda is honking at me. A police cruiser moving in the opposite direction flashes its lights.

"Move the limo now!" a voice commands over the loud-speaker. "Move the limo now!" Suddenly the Chins throw the suitcase back into the car, slam the door, and take off, scrambling awkwardly down the embankment and disappearing under the freeway underpass.

I pull forward and grab my radio.

"Goddamn it, Ruthie. They bolted on me."

"Who? The little green men in your head?"

"My fare. My fucking Chins. They just dumped out of the car."

"Did they pay?"

"No, they did not pay!" I scream. Company policy: if a driver fails to collect a fare, the driver is responsible for said fare.

Another sound comes from the suitcase. It's louder now, like the wail of a feral cat.

"Something's in their goddamn suitcase, Ruthie."

But Ruthie's moved on to other things. She's calling out a pickup in Malibu. It's a big fare, and two drivers start in on who's the closest.

At the next red light, I turn around and look at the suitcase lying on the back seat. I reach back and rap on it. No sound. Okay. Batteries dead. Fine. But then I hear another muffled cry.

I pull a hard right off Sepulveda, cross over the freeway, and start to thread my way into the dark hills on Mulholland. I find a small outcropping on the side of the road, some unofficial scenic stop. I head towards the edge of the cliff, braking when I see the grid of lights down in the Valley below me. With the car lights on and the motor running, I pull the suitcase from the back seat and lay it carefully on the ground. It's an old-style suitcase and I have to push the metal tabs apart so that the clasp flips up. My heart feels as heavy as a basketball, and after I finally get up the nerve to pull the tabs, I jump back in the car and slam the door. The suitcase doesn't open. Whatever is in there hasn't moved. I turn off the ignition and get out of the car. I find a stick in the bushes, hook it through the suitcase's lid, and lift it open. I hear somebody scream "Oh, my God! Oh, my God!" but then I realize that the sound is coming from me. I look down. Inside the suitcase is a baby.

The baby is almost new, maybe one or two months old. It's lying on a soiled yellowish cloth, making weird stuttery noises that don't exactly sound like breathing. A small tank lies next to it, and an oxygen mask that must have once covered its nose and mouth hangs down around its chin. A rank, rotten smell reaches me, and I see that the baby's legs are caked with mustardy shit. I run over to the trees and puke.

After I pull myself together, I grab the jacket I keep stashed in my trunk for cold nights and go back to the suitcase. The baby stares up at me with eyes as dark as black beans. I must be a monster to this kid. I pull the mask off over its sweaty head, lift the baby up, and cover it with my jacket. It weighs no more than a chicken and goes all limp and floppy in my hands. I have to keep it close to my chest so that it doesn't slip.

When I finally get the jacket tucked around the baby, I hold it out and take another look. It's awake, but its eyes wander off to the right as if they're tracking some lazy fly. Then its face seizes up in a look of pain and, just as quickly, relaxes. Its eyes close.

I get this hot tingling sensation all over my body, the way you do when your gut realizes something before your head does: the baby's dead, I think. I hear myself moan out loud. I hold its body up to me again, its stink clouding my nostrils, my tears wetting its face. Then I feel air against my cheek. The baby is not dead, but it's as close to it as I am to its reeking stench. In a second, I have the baby in the car, strap it as best I can into the front seat, and I'm flying down the hill.

At the emergency room, the doctors treat me as if I were a criminal. They grab the baby and disappear behind a wall of green curtains. A nurse looks at me the way some of the teachers in high school did. She probably thinks I'm the one who did this to the kid. I look around. The room is full of people slumped in yellow plastic chairs, staring off into corners. One man is pressing a bloody rag to his arm. I find a seat, but another nurse comes to tell me that I have to wait in a different room. I can come on my own, she says, or security can escort me. Two guards in uniforms stand behind her, their hands casually crossed in front of their stomachs.

The second time my mother tried to kill herself, she used a razor blade to cut her wrists fifteen minutes before I was scheduled to go over for dinner—which gave me some idea of how serious she was. When I got to the house, she was standing at the bathroom sink, running water over her wounds.

"You'd think there would be a lot of blood," she said. Pink liquid ran over her forearms and into the cracked porcelain basin.

"You missed the vein," I said, lifting her arms out of the water and wrapping a towel tightly around the one she'd managed to cut into.

"I'm just a chickenshit, I guess," she said.

I led her over to the bed, and she sat quietly for a long time as I held her arms, putting pressure on the cuts.

"You know," she said finally, "when it comes down to it, it's very difficult to kill yourself. The whole time you're doing it, your body is going 'No! No!' and you're going 'Yes! Yes!' "

"If you really mean it, you use a gun."

"Oh," she said, shuddering, as if the idea made her think of snakes or spiders. "I could never fire a gun."

"Then we're in luck."

I took off the towel. We watched a pearl of blood bubble up from the wound.

"I'm going to have a scar. I'll have to wear long sleeves from now on."

"You should have thought of that first."

"I'm not very good at thinking ahead."

I felt a fissure open up inside of me like one of those cracks in the sink. "You get by," I said. "You do okay."

"I lose things," she said. "Then I regret it but there's nothing I can do."

I had no idea what she was talking about. "You worry too much," I said. "And about all the wrong things."

"What are the right things to worry about?"

I stood up and got a box of Band-Aids from the bathroom cabinet.

"This is all you have?" I say, waving a *Star Wars* Band-Aid in the air.

"They were on sale. I guess the craze has died down."

"Well, there's one thing you don't have to worry about," I said. "No more Boba Fett fanatics on Hollywood Boulevard."

She smiled and cocked her head to the side, as if to admire me from another angle.

"Stay for a while," she said.

"Eventually I'll have to go."

"That's always the way."

The detention room is actually a closet. Inside is a metal table and a couple of chairs just like the ones in the waiting room. I try the knob; the door's locked from the outside. The only air comes from a ventilation grate high up above the door. Somebody has left a copy of a fitness magazine on the table, as if you might want to tone up on your way to prison. I flip through it and read about busting flab.

About half an hour later, a cop comes in. She's young. She's taken a lot of time on her looks: her hair is done up in a neat twist, and she wears eye shadow. She has two gold posts in each ear. She asks me a lot of questions. Who am I? Where do I live? When did I have the baby?

"It's not my baby."

"We can have you examined."

"Fine. Examine me. I've never had a baby. I'm tight as a drum."

"Don't be nasty," she says.

"Let me tell you where I got this baby."

"Tell me."

I tell her the whole story. She doesn't believe a word I say. I tell her to call Ruthanne. I tell her about the cop at the traffic accident. She asks for his name. I don't know it. I tell her where I left the suitcase on Mulholland.

"Did you get a good look at the baby?" I ask her, when it becomes clear that nothing I'm saying is convincing her. "It's fully Asian."

She looks at me blankly, as if the logic escapes her.

"You think I'd stick my baby in a suitcase and then bring it to the emergency room?"

She shoots me back a look that says I better shut up before I sink myself. I realize how serious this is, how close I am to getting arrested, and how there is nothing in my life—no person, no past—that will make me seem legit.

She takes some notes, says something unintelligible into her radio, then leaves the room.

After what feels like a long time, the cop comes back in with a man in a suit. A badge hangs off his lapel. He introduces

himself to me; he's from Immigration. He's holding the suitcase. He lays it on the table and takes out his own notepad.

"Is this the case you found in your car, ma'am?" the man
says, writing on a pad.

"Yes."

"You're sure?"

I have the feeling that if I say the wrong thing, I'll be shoved
up against the wall with my hands behind my back.

"It ought to have a tank inside," I say. "An oxygen tank. I
took it off the baby when I found him. Or her. I don't even
know what sex it is."

Neither of them answers me. The man nods at the cop, and
she puts on plastic gloves and opens the case. A rancid odor
rises up out of it, and the cop and the man reel. The soiled
blankets are balled up in the corner. The tank is there with its
tiny mask, looking sinister, the way all hospital equipment
does. I hear a small moan, and for a minute I think my mind is
playing tricks on me and I'm hearing that baby again. But
when I look up I see that the cop has her hand over her
mouth and she's crying.

I visited my mother once at her desert community. Everyone
smiled and hugged me all the time. She's happy there; she now
believes that all her breakdowns happened for a reason. If she
hadn't lost it in Texas, for instance, we'd never have made it
West, where she'd have the opportunity to lose it in L.A. It's
disaster justification.

When she decided to move, I went to her house in Laurel
Canyon to help her pack. She didn't have much—mostly

clothes, a few worthless pots, and pictures. The rest of the furniture had come with the rental.

"You move around as much as we do," she said, "you learn to live light."

"I'm not going anywhere."

She looked at me. "You like it here, don't you?"

I shrugged. "It's no different than anyplace else. So what's the point of leaving?"

"I wish I felt that way. I really do. But somehow, after a while, a place starts to feel like a splinter to me, you know? Like something you have to get rid of before it gets infected."

"I remember Florida," I said. "The electric eel at the aquarium. That was Florida, right?"

"Um," she said, distracted by packing. Or maybe she was packing to be distracted.

"And Washington, right? And Texas? That man who tried to get you to ride a horse?"

"He was a fool, that's for sure," she said.

"Cleveland was cold. Remember that man and the girl at the coffee shop?"

The look that shot across her face startled me. It made me think about all the people she must have dropped along the way. And then I thought: I really have no idea about the things that went on in my life.

"You have some memory," she said finally.

"Who were they, those people?"

"Strangers."

She didn't say anything else for the rest of the time we

packed. I felt the way I always had—that I couldn't ask more. I'd reached the limit of what she could give me, or wanted to.

When we were finally done and her bags had been stuffed in the small car, she took my face in her hands.

"I'm going to forget everything that's ever happened to me," she said, smiling. "My life begins now."

I'm standing in the parking lot outside the emergency room. People move between cars, coming and going. It's after midnight, and all this activity stands out against the hour. Bad luck happens day or night, but things that happen at night can trouble you to the core. On television, you see pictures of fires against the night sky and it looks like there's nowhere to run. A nighttime blackout leaves you bewildered and alone. The baby was a girl. They told me that much once they let me off the hook. It was a baby girl and it's likely she was for sale. Maybe the Chins—that's probably a fake name—were going to make the money, or maybe they were just the ride, taking her from one place to another.

In either case, some mother gave that baby away. Maybe she needed the cash, or maybe she thought her baby would do better without her. Maybe she'd once seen a postcard of a palm tree or a movie star and thought that in Los Angeles, USA, her little girl would find paradise.

ABOUT THE AUTHOR

Marisa Silver's short fiction has appeared in *The New Yorker* and the *Georgetown Review*, among other publications, and has been anthologized in *Best American Short Stories*. She lives in Los Angeles.

Available in Norton Paperback Fiction

Hester Kaplan	*The Edge of Marriage*
Starling Lawrence	*Legacies*
Don Lee	*Yellow*
Bernard MacLaverty	*Cal*
	Grace Notes
Lisa Michaels	*Grand Ambition*
Lydia Minatoya	*The Strangeness of Beauty*
John Nichols	*The Wizard of Loneliness*
Roy Parvin	*In the Snow Forest*
Jean Rhys	*Good Morning, Midnight*
	Wide Sargasso Sea
Israel Rosenfield	*Freud's Megalomania*
Josh Russell	*Yellow Jack*
Kerri Sakamoto	*The Electrical Field*
Josef Skvorecky	*Dvorak in Love*
Gustaf Sobin	*The Fly-Truffler*
Frank Soos	*Unified Field Theory*
Jean Christopher Spaugh	*Something Blue*
Barry Unsworth	*Losing Nelson*
	Morality Play
	Sacred Hunger
David Foster Wallace	*Girl with Curious Hair*
Brad Watson	*Last Days of the Dog-Men*
Rafi Zabor	*The Bear Comes Home*